Mall for a Month

Week 1
Monday

K.N. ERICKSON - PHAN

ISBN:0615862462
ISBN-13:9780615862460

DEDICATION

To Michelle Lussier and Maile K. McFarland

If you hadn't confiscated my book at the mall twenty-five years ago and forced me to shop for clothes all afternoon, this book would not exist.
Thank You.

CONTENTS

ACKNOWLEDGMENTS

A gift of time.

CHARACTERS

Miel (mee-Yell)

Brittany

Victoria

David

Micah

Malachi

Cody

PROLOGUE

Christmas Morning

Miel was playing Santa Claus. Her alarm awoke her at 3:30 a.m. Despite the early hour she rolled out of bed, donned her Santa hat, and lugged a great big pack over her shoulder.

There was no fireplace or chimney, but the Christmas tree was fifty feet tall. Micah had strung hefty chicken wire to hold the stockings up. Twenty-eight bulging Christmas stockings were all evenly spaced in a circle around the tree.

Miel set down her pack, pulled out a few gifts for under the tree, and then started divvying up the smaller gifts for inside the stockings. What do you get a kid who already has EVERYTHING? Many of Miel's gifts were homemade, like poems or books.

Other Santas preceded her and she found it difficult to cram her gifts into the nearly full stockings, but somehow she managed. She worked quickly. But before Miel left she couldn't help but take one little peek. She reached up to the stocking with her name on it and felt the bulging shapes through the soft red velvet. Smiling, she reached deeper inside the sock.

Ugh! Yanking her hand back she discovered it was covered in a slimy black substance. What the heck?

She pulled her stocking down from the wire and dragged it a few feet into better light. It was heavy all right. The light revealed the reason her hand was covered in gunk. Someone had deliberately put huge lumps of watered down charcoal and other sticky substances in her stocking, ruining the gifts meant for her.

Tears started to gather and one rolled down her cheek. Who could do something so hideous? Miel pulled out lump after lump of charcoal intermingled with her gifts. Maybe she could salvage some of the items.

She turned the stocking upside down and emptied it onto the floor and it was obvious that everything was ruined. Wet and black. There were also streaks of honey and what looked like dish soap. Who would want to do this to her?

A small box still in the stocking caught her eye. The little Christmas tag attached to it was still readable. To Miel, From Cody.

Her tears and heart stopped simultaneously. She knew why someone hated her. In the last week she and Cody, the cutest guy in class, had fallen deeply in love.

Thhhhunk! An arrow zoomed by her head and implanted itself in a package under the tree. She drew an inward breath. The arrow angled down, meaning it must have been shot from the second floor of the mall.

Miel jumped up, subconsciously grabbing her Christmas stocking in the process, and ran. She was a good runner. Heading in the opposite direction from where the arrow came, she made it a hundred feet before slowing down and stopping to think.

Who would hate her so much they would want her dead? A new kind of dread crept through Miel's head. She was about to enter the nearest store to the left when she saw something moving on the ground ahead.

It was a twenty foot long snake heading in her direction.

Changing her mind she leaped across the hall, hoping that whoever shot that arrow hadn't followed her closely, and slipped inside the store on the opposite side. Running behind a counter she paused sobbing. Miel needed to lose the stocking, but not until she saw what was inside the box with Cody's gift.

Trembling, she opened it up with a gasp. Inside was an intricate diamond necklace. Considering the circumstances Miel could tell that the diamonds were the real thing. She only gave herself one brief glance before closing the box and stashing it behind the counter. It would be easy to come back and pick it up later she thought. Right now she needed to find Cody - and the quickest way to do that was to make her way to the other side of the mall.

Miel ran.

CHAPTER (-1) NEGATIVE ONE
FIELD TRIP

Three weeks earlier…

The bus floor was grimy. Miel sat there, her sweaty forehead resting on the back of the seat and her limbs dangling, moving only in response to the bumps in the road. At least her school had the decency to outfit buses properly. Canadians as a rule excelled in extreme conditions. Accustomed to cold, snowy winters, Miel's school district had buses that could be considered the 'Cadillac' of buses. This bus had fancy snow tires, chains, enhanced bumpers, a high-powered heat system and a state of the art emergency kit.

Despite the elaborate additions, the school bus was by no means any cleaner than the average school bus. After all, it was used for hockey, football, swimming, and a variety of thoroughly sweat-filled and dirt encrusted activities. Miel's stomach always hurt a little bit on these long bus rides, and they had been driving steadily for nearly three hours. They were slowly approaching their destination - Spokane, Washington.

Hot, and tired of staring at the greasy floor below her, Miel looked outside at the crisp winter scene while laying her forehead on the cool window. Three weeks until Christmas she thought. It was only nine in the morning, but the dark cloud cover gave the landscape the feel of a quiet evening. One of those rare moments when people have difficulty distinguishing between night and day, like an eclipse, Miel thought.

It had been snowing chocolate chip sized flakes for the last few hours, but there was enough traffic on the rural highway to keep the fluffy snow pushed to the side of the road. This was nothing compared to the snow in Canada.

As the white covered pines whisked by, her sleepy eyes glanced briefly around. The bus was almost like a second home to her. She spent hundreds of hours going to and from her home on the bus, not to mention the time spent travelling to sporting events. (Although she couldn't get over the grimy floors. They repelled her sense of propriety.) Miel always sat in the back of the bus close to the emergency door in case she ever needed a quick escape. Running her eyes along up and down the bus she observed her classmates in their predictable occupations.

Zoe, Hannah, and Madison were sitting in the back row with Miel. Directly in front of her sat Micah, doing homework. To his left were David, Tanner, and Luke - not participating in anything considered close to a quiet activity. Strangely enough, their good friend Cody had abandoned the three guys to sit with Brittany, Lindsey, and Molly.

Next Miel's eyes were drawn several seats down to the new kid, Nick. He and Tanner were the two tallest kids in class. There were a few empty seats surrounding Tyler. Victoria was staring out the window listening to music while the rest of the girls were chatting animatedly with the three parent chaperones. Miss Schmidt forced Nolan and Malachi to sit at the front

The three parent chaperones were experts in child rearing and regimentation. Mrs. Davis was a mother of ten children; her orders were always strict and quickly obeyed. Mrs. Walton was Pierce's grandmother and Mrs. Brandt was Emily's Mom. Miel was assigned to be with Mrs. Davis, who would most likely agree to Miel's request to shop at Barnes and Noble when they reached the mall.

After a few miles, farm fields and prairie signaled their approach to Spokane as they began to enter the suburban outskirts. Evergreen tree splotches intermixed with housing subdivisions. A Dr. Seuss like water park was covered in layers of snow, giving it a forlorn quality. More houses, more car lights, and the first stoplight in town. She remembered that there were twelve intersections before they hit the mall the last time her family travelled to Spokane.

As they approached the familiar red, yellow, and green stoplights, Miel began to stretch out in her seat. She wiggled her toes, swung her neck back and forth, then finished with a spine straightening exercise. The excitement of getting to see the "big city" was beginning to sharpen her senses. She knew this was not really the "big city" but it was a heck of a lot larger than the small town she was from.

The third stoplight brought them to an intersection with a Walgreen's, a Shell gas station, and a Fred Meyer. Miel took this time to put her sneakers on and tie up the laces properly. Despite the large snow pack, she was determined to make it to their destination without having to wear her bulky snow boots.

Glancing down the aisle she noticed Brittany and Lindsey doing the exact same thing. In fact, Brittany was wearing high heeled boots. Lindsey also had a pair of low heeled boots that were a cheaper version of the pair Brittany wore.

Despite her family's poverty Lindsey managed to imitate whatever was popular. Miel never knew how Lindsey pulled this off, but she admired her in an odd way. When they first met, Miel had written Lindsey off as a crowd following fool. Later, Miel began to realize that Lindsey was only an academic simpleton because she purposely choose to spend her time following the trends. For some reason Miel did not despise Lindsey – as she normally would dislike someone acting in a similar fashion. Something in Lindsey's earnestness rubbed Miel the right way.

Tilting her head toward the front of the bus and feeling

grateful for the privacy, Miel yawned and stretched like a cat. There were fewer cars on this part of the road as highway traffic turned into city traffic. After the suburban stores there was one last swatch of dark green trees before city lights took over the landscape.

By the time they reached the fifth stoplight in Spokane the entire bus load of students came alive - stretching, and testing their lungs with loud exclamations. The baboon like actions of her fellow classmates made Miel cringe in dismay.

Micah poked his head up and blocked her view. He grinned with a mischievous smile. She smiled back. Micah in a happy mood always meant good things were about to happen. Micah always had a plan.

"Do you remember the star charts Miss Schmidt handed out last Friday?" Micah's asked.

"Yes…" She tentatively replied and then reached for the knapsack that held her science notebook. She kept all of her schoolwork meticulously organized in her backpack. Within seconds her fingers were running across the star chart Micah was describing. As she pulled the star chart out of her bag she felt some small sandpaper like bumps she hadn't noticed before.

"Look" Micah said, as he slid his star chart over the back of the seat. He cupped his hands over the chart leaving a small space for her to peak through. Miel saw small glow-in-the-dark stars.

"Miss Schmidt gave us glow in the dark star charts and didn't even tell us!" Miel exclaimed with little restraint. Miss Schmidt was the type of teacher that loved to spoil, surprise, and demand the best from all of her students. Giving out star charts and not telling anyone they glowed in the dark was just like something Miss Schmidt would do. Miel was surprised she hadn't noticed earlier, but then she hadn't looked at the charts closely yet. Micah was one of those bright students who always discovered Miss Schmidt's hidden gems. Easter Eggs he liked to call them – an obscure video game or computer term for hidden surprises.

Micah gleamed back at Miel knowingly. He gave her a

positively impish grin and sat back down in his seat. Yet What Miss Schmidt had taught in their study of astronomy this year was tantalizing. Many afternoons Miel would arrive home from school, grab a quick snack, and get on the internet to learn more about a new Hubble picture or recent astronomical discovery because of something Miss Schmidt said in class that day.

Not only could Miss Schmidt inspire her students to take an interest in their work, she also performed miracles when it came to field trips and other expensive endeavors. In fact, Miss Schmidt had to be a miracle worker to pull off this particular field trip in hard economic times. Miel knew that Miss Schmidt put in an extraordinary amount of effort into the astronomy unit this Fall by organizing stargazing sessions and guest speakers.

Their itinerary today included a stop at Spokane Falls Community College's Planetarium, meeting with a representative from the LIGO Observatory, and a final stop at Northtown Mall to watch a 3-D IMAX presentation about the Hubble Space Telescope. Their day would be packed and they did not plan to get home until after eleven p.m.

Miel's energy began to drain with the thought of the quick-paced day ahead of her. At least she had her new headlamp that she could use to read a book on the dark ride home. She was already looking forward to the peace and quiet – as well as her new book Dragonsong. Yummy, yummy books.

Coincidently they were passing by the fifteenth stoplight in Spokane and out the window to her left was Northtown Mall and the large sign of Barnes and Noble gleamed through the foggy snow. Miel could not wait to spend her precious free time browsing the books of Barnes and Noble. Miss Schmidt had promised them one hour after dinner to walk around the mall with their parent chaperones. Miel already verified with Mrs. Davis that her group would make a quick stop at the bookstore. Everything was going her way Miel thought contentedly and snuggled back into her seat as she watched the scenery go by.

To her surprise Miel's energy level increased as the day progressed. The planetarium was spectacular and the LIGO presentation was also fascinating. The day flew by quicker than she imagined and before she knew it they were one their way to Northtown.

The class was remarkably subdued for a field trip. On the bus they had less restraint, but in public the students of Miss Schmidt's class seemed to really care about how they represented their school. It was rather refreshing even for Miss Schmidt. She seemed to glow as she walked among her eager students who were actively learning. The bus ride from the LIGO presentation to Northtown got her classmates riled up again. Students were hungry for an afternoon snack but they were saving up their appetites for movie popcorn and soda.

The bus had grown progressively stuffier from the active bodies. Snow outside came down steadily all day and Miel noted that the bus driver was starting to take the city streets a bit slower. In fact… Miel scanned the streets as they came over a small hill that improved the range of her eyesight. The city was remarkably clear of traffic for a Monday afternoon. It was only one forty-five in the afternoon and yet she could only count three cars in any direction. Their bus was following the main thoroughfares through town and she expected to see more traffic. Perhaps she was remembering her past experiences in Spokane incorrectly, but no, she explicitly remembered counting the cars with her brother on a previous trip and there had been fourteen cars at a similar intersection at two in the afternoon. Hmm…from that point on Miel watched the quiet roads carefully as they trucked through town.

The bus approached Northtown on Wellesley going east and passed the mall's large concrete up-ramp. Their large school bus would need to park in the Northeast corner of the complex. Exactly opposite side of the shopping mall from the theater and book store.

Miel counted out her money and tucked her small wallet into her new purse. The purse was one splurge she had purchased for herself.

She also wanted to get some treats for friends and family back home.

At the movies she wanted to buy an extra large popcorn for Hope, Grace, and Victoria so they could use their money for candy and pop. She also wanted to get Miss Schmidt a bookmark from the bookstore. Lastly, she needed to buy a book for her little sister and grab three other books for her Mom.

Miel's Mom had carefully counted out the money for the books and sealed it in an envelope that was now at the bottom of her purse. She just needed to keep the purse close until they made it to the bookstore. Miel was always losing important things like money unless she put all of her effort into NOT losing an item. And she hated wasting her important mind power on something so trivial as money.

She was grateful that her tennis shoes had made it through the day without getting soaked by the wet snow outside. The bus driver's name was Phil and he always drove the students up to their destination before parking the bus. Miel waited patiently as the students filed out and she ended up being the last student in line to exit. When Miel's feet hit the ground she was surprised to see that four or five inches had fallen without being plowed.

The warm wet snow stuck to her sneakers and formed while balls around her feet. Everyone shoes were covered in sticky snow as they hurried across to the safety of the mall entrance. Miel had to laugh when she saw the heel marks from Brittany's boots swerve across the concrete. Serves her right for trying to wear such stylish clothes in cold weather Miel thought.

Her classmates formed an odd bunch of hooligans, kicking at their shoes and sending balls of snow scattering across the ground. Miss Schmidt grinned with resignation and herded everyone into the warm mall.

"May I have your attention please!" Miss Schmidt projected her voice over the crowd. She was eyeing Cody, Malachi, and Luke who had already broke from the pack and started to wander without permission. They turned back at the sound of Miss Schmidt's voice. Or at least Cody and Luke turned back. Miel heard Cody mutter under his breath, "Field trips can be so lame!"

"We only have five minutes to walk across the mall to the theater, buy our tickets, get snacks, and seat ourselves before the movie starts at two o'clock. I know that we will probably have ten minutes of previews to cushion our arrival, but I want us to try and be on time!" Miss Schmidt paused to grab her breath and then turned to David.

"David, would you please organize the ticket purchases? Here is the envelope with the American money. I asked Madison to be in charge of the 3-D glasses and she'll distribute them after you sit down in the movie theater." Miss Schmidt then turned to the chaperones. "Mrs. Brandt and Mrs. Walton, will you please supervise the refreshment purchases while I follow the students into the theater to save seats?"

Next, Miel overheard Miss Schmidt say softly to herself, "I hope the theater is not too crowded."

Once again raising her voice Miss Schmidt addressed the group. "Let's go!" and pointed down the mall walkway toward Sears.

The students formed an ever-evolving blob that rushed down the hall with determination. Northtown Mall was basically shaped like a block figure 8 or an H. On the Northeast corner you had Kohl's and Nordstrom. The southeast corner belonged to Sears and Cabela's, Northwest to Macy's, directly East to Penny's, and lastly the Southeast corner was occupied by Barnes and Noble on the ground floor and the theater on the second floor. Once they reached the Sears intersection the group took a right heading west toward Barnes and Noble at the far southwest corner. Before Miel could even dream of entering the sanctuary that was the bookstore, Grace yanked her arm and they took an escalator up to the second floor where the theater entrance was located.

Once they reached the theater the students were fast and efficient in the execution of their duties. First, Miss Schmidt spoke briefly with the parent volunteers about the plans for the afternoon. As a perk for serving as chaperones during the trip, Miss Schmidt agreed to supervise the entire class during the movie so that the three chaperones could shop. It was not every day that the chaperones made it down to the big city. The free gas and bus space allowed the parent chaperones to get some serious errands completed. Miss Schmidt and the parent chaperones negotiated the number of empty bus seats needed to transport the planned purchases back home. The only limits placed upon the parent chaperones was that they could not bring back any item that would cause a fuss as they went through customs. No fruit, meat, tobacco, alcohol, or extremely expensive items. Most of the border patrol members were part of their community and were used to the "school bus shopping" that went on from time to time, but no one wanted to get stuck at the border.

Next, came Miel's favorite part of the field trip – an Imax film with treats! Very expensive treats to be sure. The large popcorn she wanted to buy for Hope, Grace, and Victoria was going to cost about ten dollars and her own candy and soda would run another nine dollars. Nineteen bucks total. Sheesh! She didn't work this hard babysitting on weekends to lose her money so quickly. Oh well, it would be worth it in the end. Miel, Hope, Grace, and Victoria, David, and Tanner were in a field trip group led by Mrs. Davis and so Miel had decided to buy popcorn for the girls of her group. She was always doing random acts of kindness for those around her.

"Let's get in line first" Miel grabbed Hope's elbow and lead the girls to the snack counter. The smell of buttered popcorn reached halfway across the mall, but now that they entered the theater the scent became overpowering. Eating movie theater popcorn usually gave Miel a painful headache, it was the closest thing she had to an allergy. Nonetheless, she could usually get away with eating a few handfuls.

"Remember, I'm buying popcorn for the girls," Miel announced as she marched up to the counter and ordered confidently. Her classmates were usually in awe of her confidence when speaking to adults or large audiences. After scanning the candy menu Miel made a last minute decision to get both a Kit Kat and a

Twizzlers. Today they would celebrate in style. Miel left her soda and candy on the counter as she took the popcorn over to the self serve butter spout. She pumped the golden liquid butter on generously and shook the bag expertly so the butter was distributed evenly. The smell actually made her kind of nauseous. Perhaps she would not eat any popcorn after all.

Having beat everyone to the snack counter, Miel now had time to pause and survey the scene. She turned around nonchalantly and reviewed her classmates. Miss Schmidt and David were finishing up the ticket distribution as the last of the students entered. The three chaperones were supervising the snack purchases in an overly mothering way. Miel was glad she made it to the snack counter before Mrs. Brandt could try and talk her out of her high sugar snacks. Mrs. Brandt was known for her zealous love of healthy food. In fact, Miel could see that Mrs. Brandt scolding Luke who was clutching a huge popcorn and several candy bars for dear life. Brittany, Cody, and Molly had become a permanent trio during the trip and Miel noticed that Lindsey was upset at being left out. Miel returned to the snack counter to get her soda and head into the theater with her friends - leaving all adult supervision behind.

CHAPTER ZERO
IMAX

David finished handing out the tickets as Miss Schmidt organized the receipts. Their teacher looked tired from the long day as did everyone else. Despite fatigue, the entire class was enthusiastic about each stop on their astronomy tour. It took a teacher like Miss Schmidt to orchestrate and inspire such a learning experience, which is why David admired her.

Finished with the tickets David and Miss Schmidt had their stubs torn at the gate. It made David uneasy that there was no one else in the theater foyer. The mall seemed eerily quiet. As they walked from the bus to the theater David only counted maybe thirty people and he had expected to see at least fifty or sixty. Yet, it was a quiet Monday afternoon and the roads were icy. The people in Spokane must be terrible drivers if they couldn't handle a little snow and ice he thought.

Shaking off the feeling that something wasn't quite right, David let himself relax so he stood at the end of the refreshment line. It was moving a bit slow, so he had nothing better to do than watch his classmates. Mrs. Brandt, one of the parent chaperones, was a health food freak, she talked with anyone who would listen to her, trying to persuade them not to buy sugary food. The other two chaperones smiled in the corner as they purposely stayed out of the controversy. The two chaperones were edging their way to the back of the theater poised to go shopping. Finally Mrs. Brandt saw her friends waiting expectantly and she gave up on her health food crusade to join them.

Miss Schmidt instructed the three chaperones where to meet after the movie and then hurried back to the students. With a quick glance she realized that half the class had gone ahead into the movie without asking her permission. David, who observed everything, was anticipating her request.

"David, do you mind grabbing me a small popcorn and a Coke? I think I need to go on ahead and make sure the class is not bothering anyone in the movie theater."

"Sure, no problem," David replied as Miss Schmidt handed him twenty dollars to pay for her snacks. He also caught the implied but unspoken request; Please make sure the other students make it to the movie in one piece. David had no problem buying her snacks, and after all, the class was not really that disobedient.

David waited patiently at the back of the line as everyone made their purchases. There was only one employee at the snack counter so the line moved slowly. He may not make it into the movie until after the previews. David really liked seeing the previews so he was disappointed.

Shifting positions unconsciously David's thoughts wandered to their planetarium visit. He loved the entire presentation even though the technology was dated. Having tools like Google Sky on his computer at home allowed David to explore detailed Hubble photographs at his leisure. If only the planetarium at Spokane Falls Community College could find a way to incorporate cutting edge imagery into their planetarium presentation. He was also looking forward to the Imax movie they were about to see. First they had to sit through an hour and fifteen minutes of a movie about Antarctica and then they would get to see the 3-D presentation about the Hubble Space Telescope. He had high expectations for the visual effects.

David reached the snack counter and realized he had been so obsessed with watching his classmates and thinking about the planetarium that he had not decided what to get for himself. He looked over his options quickly.

His mind made up, David purchased Miss Schmidt's refreshments with her money from one pocket and then bought a small popcorn with his money from other pocket. He grabbed butter, napkins, and straws as he headed to the theater.

When he walked inside he caught the tail end of the final preview. Just his luck! He looked up and let his eyes adjust to the darkness. The class was well scattered across the best seats in the Imax theater - Twenty-eight students and one brave teacher. Hope, Grace, Miel and Victoria nabbed the best seats right in the middle. Brittany, Lindsey and Molly sat themselves up near the back row on the right while Cody, Pierce, Luke and Tanner were on the left and were waving to him now. Cody was pointing to the seat next to him. David noticed that Mrs. Schmidt had taken a seat right behind Cody.

David worked his way up the stairs and over to Cody who was waving something floppy in the air. In the dim light he couldn't tell what it was.

"There you are David – just in time." Miss Schmidt called out as she reached for her soda. David passed her the snacks and then reached around in his left pocket for her change. Finished, he swiveled around and sat down next to Cody. He was glad Cody was taking a break from Brittany and her clique. Brittany annoyed him like no one else in their class.

David reached over to take a closer look at what Cody had been waving in the air. They were crumpled 3D glasses. His friends were already wearing their 3D glasses even though the first movie about Antarctica was not in 3D. Cody handed over the crumpled glasses to David with a sheepish grin. David patiently flattened out his glasses and creased them along the right edges, then put them on and watched the rainbow rays bouncing off the low backlights. He loved everything 3D.

He wore the glasses for the first ten minutes of the Antarctica movie until he remembered Miss Schmidt was right behind them. He hoped she hadn't noticed. She must have strategically placed herself behind the entire class so that she could supervise them all at once.

Halfway through the Antarctica film Miss Schmidt excused herself to the restroom and reminded David and the guys to behave themselves until she returned. Little did she know just how rowdy her well behaved bunch could be given the right set of circumstances.

As soon as Miss Schmidt was out of earshot Luke and Malachi started making fun of the penguins with loud obnoxious sound effects and dance moves. Next, Cody began a popcorn fight with Brittany. David looked around nervously. Didn't any of his classmates ever worry about acting up so much in front of adults? It was then that he realized there was no one else in the room with their class. They were all alone! No wonder Cody, Luke, and Malachi were acting so crazy. David was in fact quite mischievous himself but never in the presence of an adult, and especially not a teacher. He was glad when Cody moved over several seats in order to get a better shot at Brittany. He didn't want to be associated with Cody's behavior and he knew Miss Schmidt would walk in any minute now. Of course, he did have a great view of Brittany as a handful of greasy popcorn landed on her shirt. She looked ready to kill Cody, but in that odd sort of way that made you think she probably liked him. Just as David predicted, Miss Schmidt walked in right when Cody was aiming his second attack.

"Cody, Stop! And pick up the popcorn you just threw! Malachi, Luke, Shhhh!" Miss Schmidt glared through the darkness and returned to her seat behind them. Cody picked up the popcorn obediently, but with a big smile only the guys could see. The class returned to near perfect behavior.

"You should have warned me she was coming back!" Cody whispered accusingly. David sighed but did not reply. Miss Schmidt was sitting close enough that he was sure she heard Cody's attempt at whispering. Cody was not very good at executing covert operations.

Sometimes David felt caught in the middle between several worlds. First off, he was Asian and so most of the teachers at school assumed he was super smart and most of the adults in the community assumed he was extremely obedient. It did not help that he was, in fact, both of these things. He often saw Miel and Micah hiding their intelligence from the rest of the class and he understood their predicament. Yet, at the same time he had grown up in Canada and was as Canadian as any of his classmates. Despite his general obedience in front of adults he did have a wild side. The only difference between himself and his friends is that he was smart enough not to get caught. Sometimes Cody's nonchalant attitude and Malachi's pure defiance riled him. In the end he played two roles, the good student who Miss Schmidt relied on to get the job done, and the partner in crime who students relied on to create mischief. So far, none of the adults had figured him out and only a few of his closest friends knew about his mischievous side.

"Bailey gets her clothes from the second hand store's dumpster!" David looked around to see who made that rude comment. His suspicions confirmed that it was Brittany. While he didn't usually pay attention to petty girl fights, it was hard to ignore how Brittany constantly picked on Bailey. Bailey was one of the poorest girls in class, but he happened to know that Brittany was not that much better off.

"And did you notice that she wears the same shirt almost every other day!" Molly chimed in. Her comment matched Brittany's for its rudeness and volume. Molly was a carbon copy of Brittany.

Sure enough, David could tell that Bailey had heard the intentionally loud whispers. She was sitting with Madison and Zoe about five rows in front of Brittany. Bailey did not turn to acknowledge the taunts, but David could tell she heard by how her posture changed. Her friend Zoe sent a scathing glance back at Brittany and Molly.

Miss Schmidt caught the whole exchange. She got up from

her seat and moved over to take a permanent spot behind Brittany and her gang, then quietly whispered a few well deserved admonishments to the girls who then turned and stared at the screen sullenly. Only Lindsey looked truly sorry, Brittany and Molly just looked upset at having their fun interrupted.

Embarrassed that he spent energy to paying attention to a stupid girl fight David turned to Cody and whispered.

"You should have known Miss Schmidt was coming back. Use your brain bonehead!"

"It was worth it!" Cody shot back. "Brittany thinks she looks so hot and I had her covered in the butteriest popcorn pieces. The grease will never come off!" David could not help but laugh after that image of Brittany soaked in butter came to mind. He also felt slightly relived that Cody was not beginning to like Brittany. David despised her so much he knew he couldn't stay friends with someone who liked the girl.

Luke injected himself into the conversation. "Do you think we can sneak off to GameStop after the movie?"

David thought for a moment then replied, "I grabbed one of the mall maps on our way here and checked out the shops. I know that Mrs. Brandt loves any excuse to stop by Hallmark…and it is right next to GameStop"

Tanner leaned in to offer his advice when he heard the word GameStop. "Yeah right! Like Mrs. Brandt would believe that we wanted to go to Hallmark!" Tanner may enjoy mischief as much as Cody but he was much more realistic about what could be accomplished. David trusted Tanner more than Cody.

"But," Tanner added quickly, "She may believe that one of our mothers requested an item from Hallmark. It seems like half of the kids on this field trip are picking up items for their moms," then Tanner paused and looked down in serious thought. "I suppose my mom always collects those Christmas ornaments that spin around. I could tell Mrs. Brandt that mom told me to pick up one for her." Tanner looked serious once again and then his face brightened. "Hey!

It could actually be part of my Christmas present for her next year! I could get a little shopping done early!" Then, realizing just how girly he had sounded, Tanner's face turned red. Tanner was more than manly enough with his tall height and athletic frame, but he was still self conscious around his friends. Cody, Luke, and David refrained from teasing him as Tanner was offering to sacrifice himself for the good of the whole in order to get them to GameStop.

"Good plan." Cody agreed, "We should also hit up Mrs. Brandt right after the movie before Brittany and Molly talk her into going to Forever 21 or Claire's."

"You could have fooled me Cody!" Luke chided, "You were hanging out with Brittany and Molly all morning!"

David grinned, he was impressed that Luke had the guts to point out this undeniable fact. Cody had been spending most of the morning with Brittany and Molly. Cody gave Luke a hard punch in the arm and sat back to watch the end of the Antarctica movie. The rest of the boys gave a brief glance to their right to make sure Miss Schmidt hadn't noticed their strategy session then returned their attention to the movie.

Thankfully, the Antarctica movie was coming to an end and The Hubble Space Telescope movie was about to start. David had nothing against movies about Antarctica, but after a recent popular penguin movie there seemed to be a million movies about the South Pole. In addition he had really been looking forward to the astronomy and 3D effects of The Hubble Space Telescope. As the second feature began the whole class seemed to quiet down and concentrate on the screen.

The 3D glasses had a calming effect on the fourteen year old students. Parts of the movie were a little dull as it covered the history and creation of the Hubble Space Telescope, but the images that came next were well worth the field trip. The movie highlighted hundreds of differently shaped galaxies in vivid color and detail. His favorite scene was where the camera panned down into a huge gas cloud where "baby stars" were being born. Only once did David briefly remove his 3D glasses to rub his eyes to give them a break, three dimensional effects tended to give him a slight headache. He checked his watch and was sorry to notice that it was almost five o'clock. The movie was not likely to last another ten or fifteen minutes and he didn't want it to end. He put back on his glasses and sat in rapt attention.

A few minutes later he felt a light hand on his shoulder.

"I'm running to the bathroom and will be right back." Miss Schmidt whispered to both David and Cody. David glanced around at the class quickly. Everyone was paying such close attention no one would notice her brief absence. Even Cody seemed not to have heard Miss Schmidt mention her departure.

The final scenes were like the finale to a fireworks show. Instead of ending the Imax film abruptly, the creators saved the best for last. Watching the movie caused him to seriously contemplate a career in astronomy. David's grades were near perfect so he could do anything he wanted with his life. Thinking about space, time, and the cosmos for a career was an appealing possibility.

After the grand finale the credits began to role. Students started to stand and move around, but everyone kept their eyes glued to the screen watching the last of the 3D effects. As the movie theater lights switched on and the credits ended, Zoe and her friends got up to stretch, blocking David's view of the screen.

David reluctantly took off his glasses and did the same. Cody, Luke and Tanner were jumping up on their chairs and Tanner pulled out his cell phone.

"I can't seem to get a working signal." Tanner said to no one in particular.

Luke, who had been watching Tanner, added his two cents. "You know, some movie theaters are purposely blocking cell phone signals so that people won't rudely talk and text during movies? That should be illegal. What if we had an emergency and needed to call 911?"

"Hey Tanner, we need to get to Mrs. Brandt before those

girls do, remember?" Cody swung his head toward the theater exit and his haircut did the Justin Bieber.

David had to cough to cover his laughter. Why did that Justin Bieber thing work so well on girls? Of course, he himself contemplated growing out his hair in the same manner. It was pretty long now and heading more in the Asian gangster trajectory than the Justin Bieber style. Time to get a haircut, he thought to himself.

Cody rushed to cut off Brittany and Molly at the theater exit. Tanner and Luke followed him forgetting all the garbage they had left behind. David paused for a moment and thought about picking up their garbage, but then shrugged off the impulse. Whenever this type of thing happened he justified it by imagining that there would be no more jobs for theater workers if he cleaned up everything. Still, he couldn't keep from taking his own popcorn tub and napkins as he left.

Cody and the guys were far ahead, so he found himself walking next to Micah in the hallway. It was darker here than the theater or the main hallway outside.

"That was pretty cool wasn't it?" David offered up a question in Micah's direction. Sometimes Micah was in a mood to talk and sometime he wasn't.

"I really liked the images of galaxies. I found the special effects surrounding the birth of stars fantastic," Micah said extra talkatively. Thrilled with Micah's social mood and similar opinions, David launched into a brief discussion about the movie's good and bad points. As they reached the well-lit hallway, they paused for a minute and allowed their eyes to adjust to the brighter lighting. That was when David started to listen closely to his classmates' comments up ahead.

"My eyes and head hurt."

"That movie was awesome! I wonder if Miss Schmidt will want us to do a debriefing essay like she usually assigns on field trips?" The comment was followed by a loud groan from several students.

"I have to go to the bathroom, make sure you wait for me Zoe!"

"Where is Miss Schmidt?"

"Ohhh! I could've watched that movie forever!"

"Miss Schmidt must be in the back of the group or something. She was sitting behind Brittany last time I looked. Or maybe she's in the bathroom?" Molly asked.

"I don't see Mrs. Brandt anywhere. I wish she would hurry so we could go shopping. We must go to the Brandy Melville store!" Brittany's shrill voice carried across the crowd. David looked around to see where Cody, Luke and Tanner were, but couldn't see any sign of his friends. Most of the kids were milling around near the bathrooms. David estimated that about a third of the students must be inside the bathrooms. This thought was entirely logical, because David could safely assume that most of his friends had consumed at least one large sixty-four ounce soda during the movie, and not a single one had got up to use the restroom during the Hubble film.

It was a long walk back to the theater entrance and he finally saw Cody, Luke and Tanner at the end of the hall near concessions. He wanted to shout out and get their attention but they were too far away. The guys were slowing down so they must have found Mrs. Brandt.

Once he turned his attention back to his friends milling around the bathroom, it hit him – where was Miss Schmidt? He ran through the sequence of events through his head. She went to the restroom once during the Antarctica movie and then left the theater again right at the end of the Hubble movie. He was surprised she would have purposely missed the end of the movie, but then adults seem to use the bathroom all the time and perhaps she wasn't feeling well. If that was the case poor Miss Schmidt, he could think of nothing more uncomfortable than traveling on the bus with a bunch of teenagers for four hours when you were feeling ill.

His initial worry about her disappearance subsided, but now he was feeling a different kind of sympathy. He imagined his teacher leaning over a theater toilet. She might be really sick.

David saw Bailey and Madison exit the bathroom and join Zoe near the drinking fountains.

"Hey Madison, did you see Miss Schmidt in the bathroom?" he asked while closing the distance between them. He knew Madison the best, and she was easy to approach.

It took a minute for Madison to extract herself from her friends and process what he was saying. She looked thoughtful for a minute and then scrunched up her forehead and replied. "I don't think so...but I wasn't really paying attention. Isn't she out here with the class? I thought she was sticking close to Brittany." Madison said this last part with a stern look. She didn't care for Brittany in the slightest. Before Madison could return to her conversation, David decided to speak up.

"Madison, Miss Schmidt left the movie about ten or fifteen minutes ago to use the restroom. Would you mind going back into the girls' bathroom and checking to see if she is there?" then pausing for a minute he added, "I'll check up ahead." He pointed down the hall to where Cody, Tanner, and Luke were waiting.

Slightly worried now, he started down the corridor toward Tanner. Cody and Luke walked around the corner and out of sight in the direction of the snack counter.

"Hey, where are you going?"

David turned his head to see who was calling him but did not slow his pace. It was Tyler, who was sitting on a bench alone at the edge of the group near the bathrooms.

"Joining Cody before he runs off without me!" he said loudly. Turning back he noticed that Tyler was getting up and starting to follow him.

David ran down the hall at a slow trot. There was no one around to scold him for running in the halls and he was an impatient walker. Up ahead Tanner had turned around and noticed his approach. He kept looking back and forth from David to the direction Luke and Cody had wandered.

"Hey Tanner, did you guys see Mrs. Brandt or Miss Schmidt?" He didn't pause to let Tanner answer, but turned around to look behind him. Tyler was making his way down the hallway followed by Molly, Brittany, and Lindsey. Tanner must have seen Brittany and the girls as well, because he motioned to Cody and Luke who were eyeing the snack counter in a curious manner.

"Psst! Luke, Cody…Brittany is heading this way." Tanner said as loudly as he could without letting the approaching girls hear what he was saying. "We need to beat them to Mrs. Brandt! I bet she is with the other moms in a nearby store." Tyler, who was always in the right place to eavesdrop, was just close enough to overhear what Tanner said.

Cody and Luke reluctantly turned away from the unattended snack counter when they realized that the girls were about to catch up. David focused on the task at hand and followed Tanner out of the theater and into the mall.

"Quick, which store would Mrs. Brandt and the others most likely be?" Tanner asked as he scanned the stores to the left. David automatically looked at the stores to the right. Cody and Luke were fast approaching them from behind but there was still no sign of Mrs. Brandt or any of the other chaperones.

To the right David saw Nike, Spencer Gifts, Baby Gap and the AT&T store. None of them were likely to house their chaperones.

Cody and Luke were breathing hard when they caught up with Tanner and David. They halted and gave one quick look over their shoulders, preoccupied with the approaching girls. Tyler was only a few feet away but nobody ever paid any attention to him anyway.

"Quick, do you see Mrs. Brandt?" Cody said out of breath, poised and ready to beat the girls at any cost. Without waiting for a reply Cody started running to the left and Luke followed. Luke trailed behind him looking in storefronts for their missing chaperones.

It was at this moment that David felt a chill run down his spine. Something was very wrong. He glanced back at Tyler, staring at him as if it was Tyler's fault that he suddenly felt so out of sorts. Tyler returned David's glare and then started walking slowly to the right looking intently at the second story mall windows.

Weirded out, David quickly turned away from the direction Tyler was headed. He didn't know whether to stop and calm down, or follow Luke and Cody. Tanner had abandoned him and he felt himself breathing hard.Strange, why would he be breathing hard and breaking out in a cold sweat? He slowed down his breathing and tried to think clearly. Flashes came suddenly. The cold quiet Spokane streets, the dark eerie afternoon weather, the quiet mall with only a handful of shoppers, Mrs. Schmidt leaving the theater to use the restroom.

Then two more thoughts came into focus and he really started to trip out. He glanced back at the theater entrance. The ticket booth was empty, the ticket taking stand was empty, and not a single theater employee could be seen at the snack counter or in the lobby. The electric board was still flashing the titles and times of each movie. The Antarctica/Hubble double feature was blinking in red with one more showing starting at five-thirty. There were no other customers in line at the box office waiting to buy tickets. Slowly, almost unwillingly, he swung his head back to look down the mall hallway. He could see Tanner and Luke peeking inside the Coldwater Creek Store and Cody must be a few stores ahead of them.

Then it hit him like a brick. He did not see a single soul inside the mall besides his twenty-seven classmates. No teacher, no chaperones, no shoppers, no employees. He shook his head as his vision began to blur. Seriously, David, you are jumping to conclusions. There was a perfectly reasonable explanation for why he had not yet seen another person in the mall.

He looked down the hallway to the right and saw absolutely no one. Determined to not freak out, David turned back to the theater and saw Brittany and her friends approaching. Behind Brittany, Molly, and Lindsey he could make out the rest of his classmates lingering in the hall next to the bathrooms. Just seeing the large group of people helped to calm him down. If the rest of the people left the mall, at least his friends had not.

"Mrs. Brandt promised us that we could go to the Brandy Melville store first!" Brittany announced in a shrill voice. He could tell she was both lying and trying to stall him. She looked behind him for any sign of the boys or Mrs. Brandt. Brittany usually ignored David and he liked it just fine that way.

"Where the heck are they?" Brittany snapped at David.

David was unsure of what to do next. He could not quite quell the pit in his stomach, but nor could he voice his suspicions. Wait, hadn't he just decided he was crazy? Nervous, he blurted out the first thing that came to mind.

"Cody went that way." And then pointed down the hall to where Tanner was entering yet another store in search of Mrs. Brandt. Brittany, Molly, and Lindsey spared no time in following the boys down the hall. They were still too cool to run, and looked hilarious walking stiffly down the hall as fast their high heeled boots could carry them without falling down.

David was so confused he almost laughed. Luckily, there was a railing behind him that he could lean on to steady himself. He was not dizzy, but he needed to reestablish his surroundings.

"Um….David?"

David did not reply to the strange voice. It was not familiar to him and he still wasn't feeling grounded. He needed to take a proper breath first.

"David!" the voice said a little more forcefully. He kept starring at the floor but everything was starting to come together. Tyler had been right behind him. It was Tyler's voice. Even if he didn't want to, he should still acknowledge Tyler. Pushing away from the railing he made his way toward Tyler's voice, although his eyes didn't leave the patterned tile floor of the mall. He followed the dark tiles.

"David," Tyler repeated patiently this time, "I think you should look at this."

David followed Tyler's voice. He took his time walking over. When he reached Tyler he slowly looked up. First, at Tyler's passive face, then his blue and white stripped t-shirt, and finally following his arm in the direction Tyler's finger was pointing.

For the life of him, he could not make heads or tails of what he saw.

CHAPTER ONE
STORM

Victoria hummed quietly to herself as she followed Miel, Grace and Hope out of the women's restroom. Tucked inside her coat pocket she fingered her iPod and flipped through a few songs until she found her favorite piano version of 'Minuet.' She never shared her iPod selections with any of her friends. They would make fun of her crazy line-up of pop culture songs, country music, and classical tunes. She even had a secret collection of hits from the eighties and some bluegrass music. In fact, Victoria loved music so much she had a hard time shunning any genre. True, terrible songs did exist, but every type of music also had its own genius.

Hope was the only other student who knew Victoria had a passion for music. Although all of her classmates were well aware that she had been practicing piano since she was three, none of them knew just how much of her life revolved around music. Victoria kept this obsession well hidden so that she could fit in with the crowd.

Hope was probably her closest friend. Miel and Grace were also pretty easy to get along with…in fact, Victoria was pleased with anyone who would just let her listen to her iPod in peace! She secretly listened to her iPod during the entire movie about Antarctica but then turned it off to watch the Hubble Space Telescope. That movie had been worth listening to!

She could feel Hope tugging on her sleeve to get her attention. Victoria pulled out her left ear bud to let Hope know she was listening.

"I think Miss Schmidt is missing." Hope said. It was obvious by the concerned frown on Miel and Grace's foreheads that they were already aware of the situation. That was when Victoria realized that most of the class was standing almost perfectly still - very unusual behavior for sure. She must have missed all the action while listening to music. Victoria pulled out her second ear bud and turned off her iPod. Miss Schmidt missing? Nah…she must just be ahead of the class somewhere.

Victoria glanced around at the students huddled together. She automatically noticed that Cody was missing. (He was so cute!) And if Cody was gone that usually meant Luke and Tanner were not far behind, and more often than not David as well. Hmmm… It seemed that Brittany, Molly, and Lindsey were gone too, but they were probably dawdling in the bathroom touching up their hair or putting on makeup. Hope was right, there was no sign of Miss Schmidt.

"Did someone check the bathrooms?" she asked Hope.

"Yeah, Zoe and Bailey checked every stall. They just walked out a minute ago and said there was absolutely no one in the girls' bathroom."

"You don't think she could be back in the theater? Maybe cleaning up after us slobs?" Victoria suggested with a hint of humor.

"Maybe," Hope responded. None of the students had really made a move past the bathroom area of the hallway. Victoria thought she saw Brittany and her friends down the hall at the theater entrance. They were too far away to hear her shout.

"She must be at the front of the theater – let's catch up." Malachi suggested.

Victoria kept an ear out for Malachi as she had noticed that Malachi was impulsive and never afraid to speak up in front of large groups. She watched as the mob of students slowly followed his lead.

They seemed to have lost their nervousness and began to talk loudly again. Of course, Miss Schmidt must be up at the front of the theater, where else would she be? The men's room? Of course not. Victoria smirked at the thought.

Victoria stayed put as the group moved forward. Hope turned around when she noticed that Victoria was not following the crowd.

"C'mon, whatcha doing back there? Hope asked.

"I'm going to run back and double check the theater to see if Miss Schmidt stayed there to clean up or something." Victoria said. She didn't really believe that was the case, but she wanted an excuse to stay behind.

"OK, but be quick, I bet the chaperones are ready to take us shopping!"

Victoria waved Hope off with a smile and turned back to enter the theater. Her real purpose was to….well, she did not exactly know what her real purpose was. Partially, she just liked being alone from time to time as large noisy groups annoyed her. She was also curious to see what an empty theater was like. Kinda of spooky she supposed; and she liked kinda spooky things.

Victoria pushed open the double doors and walked into the dark hallway. The main theater lights had dimmed in preparation for the next showing of Antarctica/Hubble. Advertisements for local businesses and random movie trivia questions were flashing on the screen. She tiptoed in, halfway expecting to see a movie employee cleaning up or Miss Schmidt on the phone with a chaperone.

Instead, everything was absolutely still except for the ads on the screen. Victoria was very curious, and she loved scaring herself, like when she was walking upstairs at her house at night and she could just swear something was right behind her. She felt that way now in the empty theater. Taking one last glance around to make sure she had not missed anyone she turned and ran for the door to catch up with her friends. She had scared herself properly enough.

She didn't pause when the bright light of the main hallway hit her pupils, she kept on running down the hall until she had caught up with her friends. They were trailing the pack of students as they approached the main entrance to the theater. Although running quickly with exhilaration, Victoria's boots hardly made a sound on the thick carpet.

"Boo!" she yelled while simultaneously grabbing both Grace and Hope from behind and they jumped a mile in surprise. Victoria broke out laughing as they turned around and began to mockingly beat her with their leftover popcorn tubs. She deserved the beating, and it was well worth it to add a little levity to this weird situation!

The class had always thought it was funny that two out of twenty-eight students were named after virtues. Grace and Hope. Miel had even once suggested that every student should be named after a virtue. Hope and Miel had then privately assigned virtue names to everyone in their class. Although accurate descriptions, some words were clearly not meant to be virtues, like when Miel suggested that Brittany be named 'Arrogance' and Molly should be called 'Dishonesty'. Accurate nicknames - but not virtues.

"Where do you think Mrs. Walton will take us shopping? Victoria asked in a half interested voice. She really didn't care, but wanted to make some small talk with her friends until things were figured out enough that she could put her ear buds back on.

"Mrs. Walton should have finished most of her own shopping by now. So…I bet she will let us pick." Grace replied. Of the four girls, Grace was perhaps the most interested in shopping.

"Miss Schmidt's not over here." came the loud and matter of fact statement from Malachi.

As she came around the corner and got a clearer view, Victoria could see Malachi taking a great interest in the snack counter. On second glance, Victoria saw that the snack counter had no attendant. With a third glance Victoria noticed that not a single movie theater employee was within view. That was weird. Maybe all three accidently went on a break at the same time. She also noticed that Malachi had suddenly lost interest in finding Miss Schmidt and had become very quiet. Victoria knew exactly what he was up to. He wanted to swipe some free candy while no one was looking! What a jerk! Oh well, he could get himself in trouble if he wanted to.

"Does anyone have Miss Schmidt's phone number?" one student asked. The crowd shook a few heads and muttered a few nos.

"Well, our next best bet is to call the parent chaperones, they must be nearby." Miel suggested logically. Pierce, Grace, and Emily pulled out their cell phones and started to dial. Victoria sat down on the theater bench and waited patiently while listening to the sounds around her. If there is one thing her musical training had strengthened it was her ability to hear. Not only was she good at listening to music, she could also pick up the slightest difference in background noise, nature, or language. She closed her eyes briefly and listened. Music filtering in from the main mall provided a light but steady background beat. To her right she could hear two different movie trailers being played from speakers above the concessions stand. Next came the barely audible beeps of phone numbers being dialed. Victoria furrowed her brows and listened more closely. Something was off and she could not quite figure out the missing melody.

That was when her ears picked up the sound of Malachi's shoes quietly retreating from the back of the candy counter. Her eyes flew open, and sure enough she was just in time to see Malachi walk around the side of the empty counter. He was now wearing his big puffy coat, which before had been thrown over his arm. Victoria couldn't prove it, but she would bet anyone a hundred dollars that Malachi had at least three king size candy bars in his coat pockets, including at least one Twix. She knew Twix was a favorite after seeing him knick one from the local gas station in the sixth grade.

She glared at him but said nothing. Malachi could be a powerful enemy and honestly, she did not actually see him take any candy.

"Any luck?" Malachi asked the crowd as a way to distract everyone from his detour behind the concessions stand. He walked over to where Pierce was gently banging a cell phone on his knee.

"I know my brother had a cheap phone, but I didn't know it was this cheap. I can't seem to get a signal," Pierce replied. Pierce's mother had insisted that he borrow his older brother's phone for the trip.

"Me either, that's weird. I had a perfectly clear signal on the bus before we arrived at the mall." Emily said.

"You mean none of you have a signal?" Miel queried. Miel was both quick and smart. Most of the class paid attention when she put two and two together. Miel then added, "Do you all have the same cell phone company? Maybe one of the towers is out of service. Still, that's pretty strange."

Without having to say anything more, ten of the students pulled out their cell phones and checked for service or tried to dial a phone number. Victoria had decided against bringing her cell phone with her. She did this partially because she was getting a ride home with Hope, so she would not need to call her parents, and partially because she had her iPod. No need to worry about carrying two electronic devices at once. She was not as attached to her cell phone as most of her classmates, but she was attached to her iPod.

There was a quick burst of fingers tapping away, and then a series of exclamations. As far as Victoria could tell, not a single person had managed to get cell service. That was odd. Now her senses were heightened and focused. First Miss Schmidt goes missing, and now there was no cell service. And what about those delinquent theater employees? She was starting to doubt her hypothesis about them all being on a break.

The students around her were getting a little nervous as well.

"I'm going to go find my mom. She must be nearby somewhere," Pierce mumbled to no one in particular and headed out of the theater and into the mall.

"Dude! Pierce, can you get a hold of your Mom?" Cody was shouting loudly from down the hall. Tanner, Luke, Brittany, Molly, and Lindsey were all returning from the main hall to the left. They were hurrying, but at a cautious pace. Cody's shout grabbed the attention of the entire class now and they started to follow Pierce out of the theater and into the mall so they could hear better.

"There is no one here!" screeched Brittany. "There must have been a bomb, and they evacuated everyone and forgot about us. We need to get out of here!"

"Calm down," snapped Cody. "Even if there was a fire, a bomb, or other reason to evacuate the mall our parents and Miss Schmidt would have remembered us. Besides, I can't smell any smoke." Cody looked slowly over the group as he waited for Pierce to reply. He did not seem to understand just how illogical his explanation seemed to be – but everyone else did.

"It could be a gas leak, there would be no smoke, but natural gas does have a rotten egg smell." Micah added. With that comment, everyone sniffed the air a little harder.

"All I can smell is Tanner farting," Luke chimed in, but his comment did not receive its usual laughter.

"Cody, nobody has cell service, we all checked," Malachi said before Pierce could reply. Pierce was still trying to dial his mom but to no avail.

Tanner decided to speak up, "Seriously guys, there was not a single person or mall employee anywhere - we checked while looking for Mrs. Brandt."

"And when we got to the food court things got really spooky! There were trays of untouched food on tables everywhere. It was like people disappeared into thin air!" Luke's voice wavered a bit as he described the food court, but then he regained his composure and continued, "I think Brittany is right, we need to get out of here and quick. Something strange is going on."

"Um, you guys are not going to believe this, but I don't think we are going anywhere soon." David's voice made the whole group jump. He and Tyler were standing a scant twenty feet away.

At first, no one could understand what Tyler and David were looking at so intently. The mall was brightly lit and the skylights above revealed a black winter night. Both boys were standing with their noses pressed to the cold glass mall windows looking outside.

The tall windows stretched all the way from the first floor entrance, which they were standing directly above, up to the top of the second floor. Most of the glass was misted over except where Tyler peering through a large hole in the mist he cleared with his sleeve.

Victoria did not hesitate. She walked around the slowing moving group and went to the opposite end of the windows to see for herself. All of her senses were now focused on what she could see instead of what she could hear. At first she could see absolutely nothing at all except for foggy grey windows. Once again, like back in the theater when she had been listening hard, she felt that something was missing. It had been a dark and cloudy winter day, and since it was after five o'clock it was not surprising that the sky was pitch black with no stars or moon. Then she figured it out - the lights were missing! Not natural lights, but the car lights and parking lot lights. Even a dense fog would not have wiped out every sign of life. Following Tyler's example she used the sleeve of her brand new coat to clear off the frost for a better look.

What she saw took her breath away. Under the fogged up glass were hundreds of tiny ice crystals, or to be more exact, what she thought was snow. Everything was so disorientating. Snow? If there was snow at her waist level on the second floor, then that would mean that the snow had piled up over thirty feet outside. Impossible!

She looked closely again. Perhaps it was windy outside and the snow had blown across the window and froze into place. Of course, if there was wind there would not be such dense fog. None of her hypothesis seemed to make any sense. Thirty feet of snow could not fall in two short hours. In fact she could think of nowhere on earth were snow would fall so quickly, except maybe the Antarctic. "What the heck?" she said under her breath.

"Look!" and everyone, including Victoria, turned to see where Emily was pointing. In just the right light the class could see thick large snowflakes falling down and piling up above chest level. The whole class huddled in for a closer look.

"There is at least thirty feet of snow outside. We are snowed in."

Tyler said simply, without emotion. David continued to stare at the window unbelievingly.

Victoria decided to add her observations to the conversation, "There are no car lights or lamp posts anywhere to be seen."

"I told you we were in big trouble. Maybe there was a big storm like in the movie The Day After Tomorrow and we are all about to freeze to death. No one came to get us because they were too busy trying to save themselves! We need to get out of here!" Brittany shrieked.

"Quit being so dramatic," Miel responded. "This is weird, but nothing like you described could have happened. There must be some logical explanation. Besides, if that was the case we wouldn't want to find a way out, we would be trying to hole up someplace with heat."

"Also, the mall electricity and heaters are still working." Victoria added. At her comment everyone paused for a minute to examine their surroundings. They could still hear the televisions running movie previews in the theater, the jingly holiday background music being piped through the hall, the smooth hum of the escalators, and loud blaring music was still raging at the Forever 21 store. All of a sudden, sounds that they would hardly have noticed on a normal day at the mall seemed out of place...because it was missing the noise of busy shoppers.

"Well, I don't know about you guys, but I want to try and get the heck out of here now!" Malachi said as he started moving quickly to the nearby down escalator. Victoria's classmates were generally a good group and the pressure of this situation was getting to everyone. She didn't blame him for getting nervous.

Several people started following Malachi to the escalator including Brittany and Molly. Victoria knew there was something illogical about their actions, especially if Tyler was right and there really was thirty feet of snow outside. Malachi would never be able to escape from the first floor level.

David must have been thinking the same thing. "Wait Malachi!

Stay within shouting distance and let us know what you find. We should send another group to a second story entrance. If the snow is only waist deep on our level we might have a better chance of escaping that way."

Malachi frowned, but seemed to agree as he walked swiftly down the escalator. "I will," he replied as he hopped off the bottom step and onto the ground floor. He did not wait for any of the people following him.

David looked around at the group and thought for a bit. "Let's break up into two groups. We don't want to run around haphazardly until we figure out what is going on. If we find a way out, we may need to move fast."

He paused again and pulled out the mall map he had snagged earlier that afternoon. David unfolded the map and allowed others to look over his shoulder. Pointing to the Sears exit he said, "The closest second floor exit is down the hall and outside Sears. That exit connects to the upper level of the parking garage. I say we split into two groups. One group will stay here and listen to see if Malachi has had any success downstairs, and the other group will check out the exit at Sears."

At first no one moved, but then slowly students started to volunteer go with David to Sears. Cody, Tanner, Luke, Tyler, Miel, Zoe, and Emily all decided to help him check the Sear's entrance. The rest of the students decided to stay at the theater. Maybe they thought Malachi was going to find a way out, or maybe they still did not believe there was any snow outside. Victoria wanted to go with the group to Sears, but she had some instinctive feeling that she could put her skills to better use if she stayed put. Personally, she thought Malachi was unlikely to find a way out.

"So guys, if Malachi finds a way outside send someone to let us know. We will be on the second level of Sears trying the exit on the south side. Our group will send a messenger if we have any luck," David paused and surveyed the group, then asked "Anyone have any more ideas?" A few people shook their heads, but no one spoke up.

Some of the students were still staring at the tall foggy windows, completely bewildered.

Victoria said a silent prayer for them as they headed toward Sears at a fast pace. That was when she realized why she had decided to stay at the theater instead of going with Malachi or David. Of the entire group, she could "hear" the best. Her job tonight, was to listen.

CHAPTER TWO
ESCAPE

"...we might have a better chance of escaping that way" Malachi heard David's voice faintly as he approached the bottom of the escalator. David might be right, but only if he was really buying into the idea of a thirty-foot wall of snow, which in Malachi's mind was ridiculous.

"I will!" he muttered in the direction of the lingering crowd. He also glanced back briefly, just enough to notice Brittany and a few other students following his lead. At least some people had common sense like him.

Malachi swung over the edge of the escalator, jumped five feet down and planted his feet firmly on the mall floor. He noticed with a chuckle that he had landed neatly on two grey colored squares.

Honestly, he thought life would be much better if every adult just disappeared. Although he loved his family fiercely, it was an awkward pride. His dad made money in shady ways and his mother was a bit of a dunce. Thank goodness he had inherited his intelligence from his dad. Other than his parents, he had no aunts or uncles to speak of, and the adults around school and town always treated him as if he had already committed a crime. Other than swiping a few well deserved items now and then, Malachi really didn't do anything wrong.

He patted his coat pocket where he had stashed six king size candy bars. What luck! He could not believe that all the movie employees had been gone. Malachi looked carefully around the room for hidden cameras and saw nothing suspicious. It actually would be pretty cool if everyone in the mall disappeared, but he doubted it. That is why he could not believe what David and Tyler had suggested. There was no way they would be lucky enough to be stuck in an empty mall.

The escalator jump put him squarely facing the mall exit, but he was still three or four stores away from the large doors. Like most mall exits, this one had two sets of double doors separated by an interior space that helped regulate temperature. Squinting, he tried to see past the first doors out into the second set into the parking lot. Victoria was right about one thing, from this distance he could not see a single car headlight, lamp post, or outside mall light. Usually the mall was lit up brighter than Christmas.

Edgy, Malachi continued on at a quick pace. Since he couldn't see through the doors he swung his head left and right looking for signs of people. Nothing.

He reached the automatic doors and they slid smoothly apart for him as he passed under the divider. See, there was nothing odd going on. The second doors would activate right about now…but nothing happened. Malachi still couldn't see through the doors. It must be the thickest fog imaginable was the only explanation he could come up with.

He was such a mix of emotions right now. Mad, confused, frustrated and embarrassed all at the same time. Above all he didn't want to make a fool of himself in front of everyone, and simultaneously he wanted to make a complete fool of David.

He tried wrenching his fingers between the doors and prying

them open but they wouldn't budge, and his fingers didn't really fit more than a few centimeters between the brush like fuzz between the doors.

Not willing to give up he jumped over to the manual doors that were on each side of the automatic ones.

"Wait…" someone behind him said. But it was too late. He swung the door open recklessly.

The sight in front of them answered all their questions immediately. There was a perfectly flat sheet of compact snow that stretched all the way from the bottom of the door to the top. Flat, white, mini crystals. It was beautiful Malachi's mind thought irrationally but accurately.

He reached out to touch it. It was cold.

"Don't" someone else behind him said. But as before Malachi completely ignored them.

He used his finger to trace an M in the icy flat surface. Bits of snow leaked out on to the ground. It was snow alright, feet and feet and feet of snow. Malachi wondered how high it went?

He started digging through the top of the snow pulling handfuls down behind him in his search for where the snow ended. It couldn't be more than a few feet higher he thought rationally. But the snow kept coming and he kept digging despite the snow that was falling into his shirt, down his neck, in his sleeves and into his socks. He had to crawl up into the small hole in order to dig any higher. Despite the murmur of protests behind him he kept on going.

He kept digging until he had formed an upward tunnel that went a few feet above the top of the door. All of a sudden he felt like he was in a coffin of ice. Freaking out he jumped back into the building half covered in snow and shivering from a combination of temperature and fear.

He looked around at his now silent classmates. Some were looking at him and some were still looking at the snow behind him. It took him a minute to realize that Brittany had been holding the manual door open for him the whole time. She let it go and it slowly swung back, stopping just short of closing by the snow he had dug out.

"Careful Malachi," Molly warned. "I wonder if the snow could be exerting enough pressure to crack mall windows?"

At this comment everyone looked up in apprehension. The windows really were frosty, not just foggy.

Brittany, who had been rather quiet ever since Malachi opened the first door, spoke up, "I told you there was an evacuation and we were left behind. Let's get out of here!"

Malachi agreed with her silently. He started to shiver with all the snow that had creeped into his neckline, sleeves, and socks. It was beginning to melt slowly. The icy windows also scared him. He had no interest in being in the same place if the whole wall of windows cracked at once.

He gulped and nodded. "Let's go."

"What about the door, shouldn't we try to close it?" asked Molly.

Brittany was already in the mall when she looked back at Molly. "Are you crazy! We could never get that thing closed. Besides, I think the windows might implode any minute. You wouldn't want to be here when that happened would you?"

"I guess…" Molly looked torn, but the thought of turning into a frozen pancake persuaded her to give up the idea and follow Brittany.

"See anything?" yelled a female voice from the second floor. Hope wandered down the second floor walkway and was leaning over the railing trying to get a clear view of the first floor entrance. Malachi yelled back as soon as they could see Hope.

"There's tons of snow piled up out there! We're not getting out that way!"

"There is no way out, all the other people left us to die!" Brittany wailed. Even Molly had to glare at Brittany for that comment. Many of the students shared Brittany's fear, but hearing it spoken out loud was not what they needed at the moment.

Malachi led the students back up the escalator at a slower pace.

He needed the time to think about what to do next; he was torn between a desire to be stranded all alone in the mall and the more logical feeling of being totally freaked out. On one hand he could imagine all the stuff that would be at his disposal if they were stuck in the mall! Even if they were only there for twenty-four hours before they were rescued he could get his hands on anything. The possibilities were endless. He even went as far as thinking about what he could steal and hide away. He could stash it in the men's room so that after they were rescued he might have a chance to come back. Sheesh, he was thinking about video games at a time when their lives might be in grave danger, he better shake off these thoughts and concentrate on the task at hand.

Of course, when he contemplated the reasons they had been abandoned in the mall, his mind only produced terrible thoughts. What if the snow was a fast acting nuclear winter produced by a nuclear bomb? Once again, an unlikely scenario, but nothing seemed to adequately explain so much snow in so little time. Then he had an idea. One explanation that seemed to fit.

He reached the main group outside of the theater at the same time as his followers. He had been going awfully slow. His group was pelted with questions as soon as they hit the second floor. Malachi let Brittany and Molly relay the details of the story as he caught his breath. Besides, he was a little embarrassed about being buried in snow and evidence of the avalanche was dripping of his clothes as they spoke. Brrr. He was getting kind of cold and would need to find a change of clothes soon. The mall was kept reasonably warm, but heat was too expensive to keep it as cozy as a log cabin.

When the girls were finished relaying all the necessary facts, and some unnecessary ones as well, Malachi decided to speak up about his idea. It was a relatively good one he thought.

"Guys, I know it seems hard to imagine so much snow building up in such little time. But what if there was a really big snow storm and the wind has pushed it in a drift against the south side of the mall? I mean, in Saskatchewan it is not unheard of to see thirty feet snow drifts in some places right? If there is a thirty-foot snow drift on this side of the mall there might only be a few feet on the north side, away from the wind. I think we should send a group over there. We can check on the west side exits while we're at it. I think there are two of them between here and Macy's."

Malachi paused and drew another quick breath. He was surprised that everyone was actually listening to him for once as usually he was ignored. "Well, does anyone want to go with me? he asked.

Malachi was surprised that Brittany and Molly did not volunteer. Now that Brittany knew they were sure to die she seemed to have other priorities. Surprisingly, it was Madison, Micah, and Nolan who slowly lifted their hands. Malachi looked toward the mall walkways to the north. It did seem strangely quiet except for the loud music blaring out of Forever 21. He usually liked the music but it seemed so out of place in the empty mall. He wished someone would go into Forever 21 and smash the stereo.

The small group started walking north on the second floor. It felt safer to be looking down on the first floor landing instead of the other way around. Malachi was positive they could not be the only people left in the mall. He kept expecting someone to jump out and surprise them around every corner.

With Madison, Micah, and Nolan along, Malachi felt a bit more reserved. He did not feel the confidence necessary to take charge like he did with the last group, so he walked side by side and silently next to them.

When they reached the middle of the mall they could see a full view of the food court the guys described earlier. Tanner was right - it looked like the shoppers must have left in a rush leaving their food and drink behind. It reminded Malachi of that one movie series Left Behind. Spooky! He sure as heck hoped that the rapture was not the reason for the sudden disappearance of everyone in the mall. What would that say about his whole class being left behind?

Madison walked over to the nearby tables of the food court for a closer inspection. They all followed her, intrigued and maybe even a little hungry. Madison gently prodded a few half eaten menu items with a plastic fork. Lastly, she picked up a supersized hamburger by the wrapper and sniffed.

"What are you doing?" Nolan asked.

"Well, I just wanted to get an idea of how long ago everyone disappeared. We were in the movie theater from two to five o'clock. Obviously, they must have been evacuated during that time period. That doesn't give us any real information, but at least we know they were probably not evacuated right at two o'clock. It must have been a little later."

Malachi's stomach rumbled loudly. He was embarrassed.

"Want a burger?" Madison teased and offered him the gooey old burger.

"Heck no!" said Malachi. While actually very hungry, Malachi did not think he was psychologically ready to eat. None of them were. He looked at Nolan and Micah, who seemed to share a similar sentiment.

"Well, let's get going, I want to be able to get out of here as fast as we can." Malachi was still not ready to even entertain the idea that they may not be able to get out at all. At least the power had not gone out. Now that would be weird!

The four turned and started walking to the east exit of the mall. They were still on the second floor so they looked briefly down to the first floor but couldn't see the mall exit below. The windows above the east exit on the second floor looked identical to those they had seen on the south side of the mall. They were foggy with ice crystals that must be snow. It seemed as though the north side of the mall may harbor their only chance to prove the snowdrift theory.

It would be ridiculous to think that thirty feet of snow had blanketed the entire mall! That would mean the entire city was buried. Most of the houses surrounding the mall were built in the 1950's and stood only one story tall. Malachi shivered as he thought about what it would be like to be buried alive in your own home. He wondered if the mall was surrounded by hundreds of people buried alive in their one-story homes.

As the four of them marched forward they seemed to naturally follow a calculated pattern. Malachi and Madison were walking on the right and they were scanning each store on that side looking for signs of life. Nolan and Micah were walking on the left. Nolan was letting his hand faintly trace the handrail as they walked, only removing it when a garbage can or bench got in the way.

"Do you guys think the electricity might go out?" Malachi asked. The thought had been troubling him since they left the food court.

"I've been thinking the same thing," said Micah.

"That would be spooky," Madison agreed, shivering. It was getting a little cold as it was.

Madison's shiver caused Malachi to remember his own chilly garments. He would need to replace these soon. They were approaching Macy's at the north corner. Macy's had one second story exit that connected to a parking garage outside.

"I think we should keep a lookout for flashlights and grab a few if we see them," Micah suggested thoughtfully as they crossed the threshold into Macy's. "We may have trouble finding batteries for them, although sometimes batteries are included."

"Good idea," Malachi responded. Micah was really smart even if his autism made him really, really odd at times. It both creeped out Malachi and comforted him to have Micah along for the trip. You just had to get used to Micah's idiosyncrasies. "Hey guys, let's check out the second floor exit first. If the south side is really just covered by a snow drift, and not thirty feet of snow, then we should have a better view from this level.

The three nodded in response probably because as they entered Macy's the quietness and vastness of the space seemed odd. Out on the walkway they still had the mall background music and music blaring from individual stores. Here in Macy's it was absolutely quiet. Usually, you could hear different departments calling one another over the loudspeakers, but not now.

Malachi had to admit that Macy's had some of the most unique mannequins. But walking through the store all alone made him feel like every mannequin was watching them, even though these particular models did not have eyes or other facial features.

They walked past the cosmetics counter and through the women's clothing section as they approached the northernmost entrance. As they got closer Malachi was not encouraged by what they saw. Just like the previous sites he could see no light penetrating the exterior. He had at least hoped they would see a light shining from the parking lot. Macy's exits also had two rows of doors separated by an open space to conserve energy, just like the main mall exits. Even though it was pitch black outside, they pushed their way through the first set of doors. Macy's did not have any automatics doors, thank goodness..

Each of them walked up closer to one of the four doors to get a better look. Imitating Tyler's earlier action, Malachi took his sleeve and cleared off a portion of the foggy door. The cold from the window practically refroze his wet sleeve. Looking out, he thought he could trace the thin line of snowpack a few inches above his head. If what he was seeing was true, that would mean that not only was the entire mall buried in thirty feet of snow, almost an entire foot had fallen since they had first noticed the snow less than an hour ago. Malachi checked his watch, it was a quarter to six.

Nolan, Micah, and Madison each followed suit and cleared a portion of the glass door with their sleeves. All were staring at the faint line of snowpack. Madison traced it across the door with her forefinger.

"Wow, I just can't believe it!" she whispered. "I have never in my life seen snow like this before."

"It's just plain weird," Nolan added. "Gives me goose bumps, and I don't scare easily!"

"Well what should we do next?" Madison asked, taking a step back from the door.

"We should hurry back to the main group so they don't worry about us, and check the other entrances before we go back. Just in case..." Nolan suggested.

"Just in case what?" Malachi shot back. He was starting to lose all hope that they were going to escape from the mall anytime soon. His thoughts were already turning to what they should do now if they were stuck. He didn't wait for Nolan to respond. "Let's go check the second floor west exit, then go down stairs and confirm that the two lower floor exits look the same, which I am guessing they will…"

He waited a second for affirmation before continuing on. Madison nodded her head and then Malachi made another suggestion. "Why don't you guys look around house wares for some flashlights while I get a change of dry clothes from the men's section?"

Madison eyed him warily and then blurted out, "You're just going to help yourself to new clothes I bet! You can't steal stuff!" She had a strong sense of honor and Madison seemed to be reading his mind.

"Madison, I am freezing to death and we're stuck in a mall buried in thirty feet of snow. I hardly doubt Macy's is going to sue me afterwards for borrowing some clothes. Besides, when we get out of here they will probably be paying us to tell our story on all the networks. So lay off!" Madison looked hurt, and Malachi realized his tone of voice had been harsh. It always upset him when people tried to lay that goody-two-shoes bit on him. They had no idea what it was like to grow up like he did with a dead beat dad and a loser mom.

Micah was watching patiently and then spoke up in a quiet voice. "If they don't have flashlights here at Macy's I know there is a Radio Shack on the lower level. It's on the way back to the theater. I am pretty sure Radio Shack will have batteries too."

"Let's go check the other second floor exit before we go downstairs," Malachi grumbled and started ahead of them in a huff. He was in a bad mood now.

They checked the exit and found it to be exactly the same as on the north side. Next, they headed to the middle of the department store and took the escalator down to the main floor.

"House wares are in the basement. You guys are not too scared to go down there alone without me are you?" Malachi asked the group in a challenging voice. He just wanted to get rid of them while he was picking out his new clothes. None of the three responded, they just gave him funny looks – Madison glared – then took the escalator leading to the basement.

Malachi regretted being separated almost immediately and broke out in a cold sweat as soon as he realized he was truly alone. He looked at one of the mannequins and it freaked him out. He had to consciously not look at the mannequins and avoided their displays by a wide margin.

Walking into the men's section he distracted himself by first looking for a pair of jeans. Malachi never really had the luxury to shop in any section he wanted. Now there was no one who could stop him. He did not know much about fashion, but he did know about money. If he was going to "borrow" a pair of jeans he might as well make them nice ones. He started walking around the denim section looking at price tags. $60 dollars, $85, $115. Wow! Even accounting for currency exchange he had never had a pair of jean costing over forty-five American dollars. And here the jeans seemed to start at sixty dollars. He kept browsing until he came to the brand with the most expensive tags, it was called 7 for all Mankind. What a interesting name, he wondered what it meant.

Still, he wanted to make the most out of this situation. He looked through the jeans quickly and found a pair he liked. They were originally $235 dollars but on sale for $195.

Pulling off the tags and stickers he tugged at the security tag and thought for a moment then walked over to the closest sales counter. It didn't take him long to figure out how to pop off the security tag.

He looked around quickly to make sure he was alone, then stripped and redressed in one fast motion. The jeans were a good fit. He pulled off the tags and stickers. Heading for the nearest trash can he threw away his old jeans, his coat, the soggy candy bars, his wet shirt, and the tags from his new jeans.

He purposely threw away his old clothes so he would be cold enough to find the new ones quickly. He figured he only had a few minutes before the crew returned from the basement. Shivering, he listened to his dirty old tennis shoes squeak as he walked across Macy's floor. It would be nice to replace those as well he thought.

Looking around, he could see that shoes were at the opposite corner of the building. He made his way in that direction, grabbing the closest warm shirt he could find and snagging a sweet Calvin Klein leather jacket. The jacket made him look the Fonz, that old school nineteen-fifties character his grandpa had shown him on TV once.

At the last minute as he was walking through accessories, he grabbed a high end leather wallet. Malachi never needed or owned a wallet before, but this opportunity was too good to pass up. Before grabbing the wallet he took a brief look around for security cameras and then pocketed it swiftly. He would have to take the wallet out of its packaging later.

He also remembered to pick up a pair of nice warm 100% angora wool socks and a leather belt before he left the accessories department. It felt so darn good to be picking out items because you liked them without regard to price. He could get used to this.

Shoes were an entirely different matter. Malachi had always dreamed of having an expensive shoe collection. Whether it was a basketball player, a lawyer, or a successful business man, shoes seemed to make the man.

He had picked out his other items quickly so that he could really take his time finding the right shoes. But then a thought struck him. When picking out shoes at a department store the shoe salesman always asked what size you wanted and then went and got a box from the back. He was only used to shopping at stores where all the sizes were stacked right in front of you. This was going to be a touch more complicated than he originally planned, especially if he was going to get the shoes on before his friends came back upstairs.

Quickening his pace, Malachi walked over to the tennis shoes.

While getting a good pair of boots might be more practical back home, Malachi really just wanted a pair of tennis shoes. Once again, he could not help but let the price be his guide. He found a few pairs of Nike and Adidas that were a little over $150.

He grabbed the display shoe and made his way back to the shoe storage area in the back. Passing by an "employees only" sign Malachi started to feel pretty cool. He pretended to be a salesman with a big walk, both for the fun of it, and to calm his nerves. Back in the storeroom it was even quieter, and he realized that if anything ever happened to him his friends would not likely look back here.

While looking for his size in the storeroom Malachi was reminded that there were lots of back rooms in a mall that non-employees never entered. He knew there were several back walkways whose doors were covered by signs that read "Mall Employees Only.' Most of those doors seemed to have some sort of keypad or lock. If they were stuck in this mall longer than twenty-four hours he would be sure to explore those passageways. Then there must be mall offices for management, security, and maintenance. A whole labyrinth of unexplored places.

"Malachi!" He heard his name being called by one of the guys, but it was so muffled he couldn't tell if it was Nolan or Micah. Dang it! He would have to hurry and find his shoes before they started to worry. Maybe they would take the time to check the changing rooms?

He stumbled upon the Nike section and he decided to get that brand. Using the pictures on the side of the boxes, it was relatively easy to spot the shoe he was looking for. Now, if only his luck held and they had his size. Score! Right at eye level he found the size nines. He pulled the shoes out of the box, yanked out the inside stuffing, and tried them on. They still had that stiff new shoe feel, but that was to be expected. Lacing up the sneakers he ran up the aisle leaving his old shoes and the packaging behind him in the middle of the floor.

He felt good in his new shoes, jeans, shirt, and jacket. That was when he realized he still had his old boxers on. Ah well, he should have snagged a pair earlier, he just hadn't been thinking.

"Over here guys!" he hollered across the wide space. He could see the three of them milling about in the men's clothing section. Sure enough, Nolan was actually looking in the changing rooms for him. Malachi trotted over to where they were standing.

On the way he caught a glimpse of himself in a full length mirror. Malachi never cared for his appearance before, but he had to admit he looked kind of cool in these new clothes. One day, when he had money, he would spend more time picking out his clothes.

"Did you find any flashlights?" he asked. Then he realized the question was basically a moot point because they were obviously empty handed. They were all staring at him, but Madison was the only one that looked furious.

"What the heck do you think you are doing stealing all those fancy clothes! You should put them back right now. They are not yours!" She then folded her arms and stared him down. Nolan and Malachi didn't say a word.

"Shut-up Madison and mind your own business. My clothes were soaked to the bone. If I get in trouble I will deal with the consequences," he replied hotly.

"You could have at least picked out something less expensive. Those jeans are worth at least a hundred bucks," Madison said.

"Mind – your – own – business!" He said through a clenched jaw. Malachi was really upset now. At least Madison didn't know they were really worth two hundred dollars.

"We should be getting going, " Micah interjected, "I want to stop by Radio Shack on the way back." Micah was always black and white about what needed to be done. He rarely involved himself in the petty dealings of his classmates.

They walked out of Macy's with Madison trudging sullenly behind. She wasn't gonna let up on him was she? He happened to know that Madison came from one of the wealthiest families in town. What right did she have to judge him for getting some warm clothes? That was when he also realized that Madison never seemed to wear fancy brand name clothes. She always had nice ones, but nothing extravagant. He wondered what it would be like to have lots of money but not use it. Malachi just didn't get Madison, or girls in general.

As they walked along he noticed that Nolan seemed to be looking at him enviously out of the corner of his eye. Well, at least one person understood why he would want to wear expensive clothes. He may never have another chance like this in his life.

Malachi stared intently as he passed by Famous Footwear, Whiz Kids, and Baby Gap. Radio Shack was on the left just a few feet ahead. Malachi watched Micah made a beeline for the store.

Malachi followed as Micah expertly searched the store for flashlights. Micah scanned, shifted a few items, frowned, and then finally pulled something off the shelf. Next, he walked through a little half door to get behind the check-out counter.

"You gonna rob the place now?" Malachi asked Micah in jest. He was still upset at Madison. He would do anything to direct the attention away from him and he knew this would work. Micah always took jokes literally, even when he logically knew it was humor.

Micah glared at him then proceeded to ignore him, first looking through the battery display until he found the basic AA and AAAs. Swiveling around, he licked his finger and picked up a plastic Radio Shack bag and filled it with several packets of different batteries. Finished, he walked around and joined the group. Malachi was watching him the whole time.

"What? You aren't going to accuse Micah of stealing are you? Miss high and mighty?" Malachi sneered at Madison. She locked eyes with him and did not flinch. He turned away and addressed Micah to avoid her gaze.

"What did you find?"

"There were a few small flashlights as well as some individual head lamps. I think Sears will have more of a selection if the electricity does go out. They have larger and brighter flashlights, including some industrial ones." Micah replied without pausing to talk, but kept on walking as he replied to Malachi.

Everyone seemed to feel the need to return to the larger group. Malachi had an uneasy feeling that the other students might find a way out of the mall and leave the four of them behind.

"Wait a minute!" Nolan turned around and ran back into Radio Shack. He returned holding several large plastic packages.

"Do you have lots of AAA batteries Micah?" he asked.

Micah nodded in affirmation.

"Then we might be able to make use of these." Nolan held up the packages so everyone could get a good look. He was holding six sets of long range Walkie Talkies.

"Brilliant!" Madison exclaimed. "I wish we were using them right now. Let's hurry and get back."

They walked together down the mall walkway in silence, no longer accompanied by the squeaking of Malachi's formerly wet sneakers.

CHAPTER THREE
WAIST HIGH

Cody was glad to be following David, Luke, and Tanner to check out the Sear's exit. He was not sure what was going on with the snow, but he sure as heck knew who he wanted to be with when the going got tough. And although things did not seem too bad at the moment – after all, there were worse things than getting stuck in a mall – he sensed the situation could get much worse.

For the most part, if Cody followed his instincts, life went pretty smoothly for him. Other than getting poor grades in school he was at the top of his game in every other aspect of his life. He had a great family, a good weekend job, he was talented at sports, and girls loved him. He was charming enough that most everyone liked him even the teachers that wished he put more effort into his studies. Oh well, he couldn't help it that he didn't like to read!

When he was with David and the guys he could pretty much let down his guard and enjoy the ride. David was the most responsible of the group, Luke did a bunch of the deep thinking, and Tanner was their moral compass. Cody meanwhile was the jokester, the prankster, the girl magnet, and he was proud of it.

So as their group walked east along the mall walkway towards

Sears, Cody did so with a light heart. He was not really too worried about their situation, as there must be some logical explanation for the snow. And like any twenty first century kid growing up with modern media he pretty much expected that they would be rescued quickly without suffering too much pain or heartache. What is the worst that could happen? They spend forty-eight hours stuck in a mall surviving on candy bars and old theater popcorn while huddled in blankets? As far as survival situations went, getting stuck in the mall was a much better prospect than being stranded in the Sahara or Antarctica.

As they passed GameStop he couldn't help himself, he just had to have one peek inside.

"C'mon Cody, we need to hurry up and stick together." It was David's voice alright. Cody had been expecting that.

"No worries, I'll catch up in a second. Go on without me." said Cody.

David kept the group walking, so Cody took David's warning seriously. He ran into GameStop and glanced up to find the PS5 section and then skimmed the titles. He took a second to look at the store around him. Usually when he visited GameStop he was always too shy to do anything other than focus on one small section at a time, the overfriendly staff made it difficult to look around the store. Now that he was all alone in the shop he could take it all in with one slow look. He even closed his eyes and breathed in the sweet smell of plastic and overheating game consoles. His hands itched to reach out and play the latest demo set. Although he was lucky enough to have a PS4 at home, he really wished he could afford the other game systems as well.

He had taken too long. Judging by the amount of time he had spent in GameStop, David must be waiting for him at the Sears entrance. Letting out an uncharacteristic sigh…Cody turned and walked out of the store. Someday, he promised the games silently. Someday I will return and give each of you the proper attention you deserve.

Just as he predicted David and the group were waiting for him down the hall. Cody tried to make up for his transgression by breaking into a full sprint to catch up with them.

"See? It only took me a second." Cody flashed his smile at the entire bunch and he always reserved the tail end of his famous gaze for the ladies. He thought he saw both Zoe and Miel blush just a little bit. They were not the flirting type, but Cody spared no female his charms. It worked particularly well on old ladies. Cody was not chauvinistic about it, but his mother had taught him to appreciate all women and his father had taught him to treat them all like queens. Their combined parenting styles had resulted in the creation of a heartthrob. His vague resemblance to Justin Bieber did not hurt him one bit.

As they walked into Sears, Cody took on a more serious attitude. He didn't want to annoy David too much. Cody also had a pretty good sense of direction so he started keeping tabs on where they were going and he glanced at the Sears map on the way in. The second floor was almost completely clothing and women's accessories like make-up, jewelry, etc. Downstairs housed tools, appliances, electronics, kitchenware, and a bedding section. If they ended up being stranded in the mall after hours Cody figured there would be enough beds in Sears to sleep them all comfortably. He thought there might also be a specialty bed store somewhere in the middle of the mall.

They walked through the lonely aisles of clothes and shoes and made their way to the west exit. Sears was connected to the mall on the north side and by a second story parking garage on the remaining three sides. David was leading the group, and Cody suspected David wanted to check the snow level before moving to the south entrance.

David was fast in his evaluation. Cody watched him duck into the entryway area using the manual door. He must be avoiding the automatic doors. David was so quick that nobody tried to follow him. They could see him peering into the night through the foggy glass. David came back out in a rush and reported his findings.

"The snow level must be between four and five feet. But I think I see the lights from the top of the parking garage. Let's hurry to the south entrance. Maybe the snow is a little less deep there, and either way, that is where I told everyone we would be," David announced.

"You know, David, if we are going to try and get out with all that snow we might need to grab some gloves and shovels. I would be willing to run downstairs with Tanner to look for shovels," offered Luke.

"Great idea – you need to hurry though. I could faintly see the snowflakes still flying. I am not sure how far we can make it or where we would go. But we might as well try," David replied.

"Zoe and I will go looking for warm hats and gloves. I see them right over there." Miel pointed to the middle of the store where men and women's winter accessories were conveniently located side by side.

"Sounds good!" David actually smiled through his frown, "Just don't take more than five to ten minutes without reporting back. I have a feeling we are going to need to move fast if we have any hope of escape.

The kids split up and moved in opposite directions. Cody decided he would much rather go with Luke and Tanner to the tool section. David could fend for himself.

"Wait up guys, I'm coming with you," Cody called out to Luke and Tanner.

"Sweet," Luke and Tanner replied in unison. Sometimes, Cody thought, those two were inseparable.

They snaked their way through the jewelry and perfume section and headed for the west side of the building where the escalators were. Weird. All of the escalators were still running. It just didn't seem right that if there were no people in the building that the escalators would still be moving. Cody had seen enough movies, and been to enough malls, to know that the escalators were turned off when the stores closed at night.

Then he looked around at the brightly lit store, the unlocked building, and remembered the food court full of half-eaten food. The people who left this place left in a hurry…or disappeared into thin air.

He followed Tanner and Luke in a breakneck run down the escalators. The guys had pent up energy after sitting all day, and recent events had pumped up their adrenalin. They reached the bottom of the stairs and looked around.

"Tools are this way," Luke motioned to the south.

"Wait," Cody interjected, looking to the north. "See? Behind the exercise equipment! I think the winter shovels are kept over there."

"Oh yeah, okay."

Since the winter season was still in full swing, Sears set up a winter display with all types of snow removal equipment.

Tanner went straight to the shovels and started to pick up five or six of various sizes and styles. Luke and Cody were looking over the entire selection to see if there was anything else that might come in handy.

"I might get some buckets and rope from the general tool section," Luke said.

"Good idea, Tanner and I will keep looking here." Cody replied and then added with an impish smile, "be sure to watch out for the boogey man!"

Luke punched his arm hard in response. Cody felt bad about teasing him, but he just couldn't help himself whenever the opportunity presented itself. Besides, Luke was no scaredy cat, so the warning would just keep him on his toes while he was alone in the tool section. Besides, the tools were only a few feet away.

Luke headed out and Cody watched as Tanner comically tried to add more shovels to his load.

"I could use a little help here Cody."

"No way!" Cody replied in a distracted tone.

Tanner looked back over his shoulder at Cody, "What is it Cody?"

"Snow blowers!"

"Huh?"

Tanner and Cody both turned their heads to look at the row of shiny new snow blowers displayed strategically along the main aisle.

"That is the best idea you've had in years!" Tanner said, and dropped all seven shovels causing a loud crash. They both started checking out different models and reading the specifications on each box.

"It will need to be an electric powered snow blower - I don't know where we would get gasoline in the mall." Tanner commented.

Cody nodded and kept looking. "Well, if we're going to move a snow blower up to the second floor we might as well pick a decent one." After looking at two or three versions Cody picked one out.

"I think this is it Tanner," he said pointing at a red and black one.

"What do we need to make it work?" asked Tanner.

"Let's see, most of that info is usually right on the box, and if not, owners' manuals are tied to each of the floor models." Cody looked closely at the box. "It says here on the box 'use with a 16-gauge outdoor extension cord.'"

"16-gague extension cord." Tanner repeated as he ran toward tools in search. "Hey Luke" he shouted "we need a 16-gague extension cord."

"What did ya say?" Luke hollered back.

"Never mind," Tanner had just spotted and entire row of extension cords. Reaching out he grabbed one, and then two more.

"Bring them over here bro, and we can see if this floor model works, otherwise we might have to open a new one and it may not be pre-assembled." Cody said.

Tanner and Cody were putting together several hundred foot extension cords when Luke came back. He was carrying two heavy buckets filled with a variety of tools.

"What are you guys doing? We'd better get upstairs soon, you heard David say ten minutes."

"Yup, just let us give this a try." Cody replied. "We may have a working snow blower!" Honestly, Cody was proud that the snow blower was his idea. He wasn't usually the one to come up with the good ideas.

"Awesome," Luke replied and set down his buckets. He quickly realized what else was needed. "There should be an outlet nearby. They're all over the place in a big store like this, and there should be one under the cash register." He walked behind a nearby counter. "Here we go, throw me the plug."

Within a few seconds Cody started up the snow blower. It purred, and the loud sound echoed across the store. He hoped they weren't scaring their friends upstairs. Cody let out a whoop.

"Let's go guys! I think I can push this up using the escalator. There is an elevator somewhere in the back, but we don't have time to search for it."

After helping Cody string the extension cords around the snow blower Tanner picked up his pile of shovels and Luke grabbed the buckets. They made their way to the escalator.

"Whew! The snow blower is just the right width for an escalator. Now, I am going to try and tip it back like I see mothers do with their baby strollers...and we're in business guys!" Cody could not hide his excitement. The snow blower might save the day!

CHAPTER 4
SHOVELING

"Sounds good!" David actually smiled through his frown, "Just don't take more than five or ten minutes without reporting. I have a feeling we are going to need to move fast if we have any chance of escape."

The kids split up and moved in opposite directions. Tyler and David headed straight for the south side of the building. Miel and Zoe headed for the hats; Cody, Luke and Tanner the escalator. When Tyler and David arrived at the glass doors both boys went inside the manual door avoiding the automatic door. They seemed to be thinking the same thing. If the automatic doors were to open they may not be able to keep the snow out. And in a worst case scenario, they would want to keep the mall as warm as possible - especially if the electricity stopped working.

Tyler and David inspected the door quietly. Just as before, they used the sleeves of their jackets to clear off a space on the foggy window.

"Hey! It's not so deep here!" David managed to say first. He and Tyler noticed at the exact same time – the snow was only a few feet high out this exit. Tyler and David opened the door outward carelessly. They still had to press hard in order to squish the snow, but using their combined strength they managed to open the door a full ninety degrees. Finally cautious, they stared at the scene before them. Wind pushed a small stream of snow into the through their feet and onto the carpet.

The section of the walkway leading out to the top level of the parking garage was covered by a roof. The snow only managed to drift to a level of two feet in most places, leaving a small but manageable trail out to the parking garage. Even with this good news David could tell that the snow was piled up quite a bit higher once the roof ended at the wide open top level of the parking garage.

Tyler spoke up, “You know, even if we manage to make it to the parking lot, what next? The parking lot has three levels. We might be able to make it down, but it would only be an ice cave as the whole area is covered in snow. And if we made it to the edge of the parking garage what would we see? We are surrounded by blocks and blocks of one story houses that must be completely buried. Even the few two story commercial buildings I saw on the way here were half the height of this mall. We are probably standing on the highest building for miles around as far as I know.”

David mused for awhile. Tyler had brought up some good points he had not thought of in his rush to find a way out of the mall.

“I agree. I suppose the only real reason for trying to dig our way out will be to thoroughly assess the situation outside.” Then another idea came to him. “If this really is like that movie The Day After Tomorrow there might be National Guard helicopters looking for survivors. We could dig our way to the top of the parking garage and set up some kind of signal in the morning.” David suddenly realized what he said. He was slowly coming to grips with the idea that they may not be rescued this evening. It might take several days to get out of this mess and he only hoped the temperature did not drop too low.

Tyler nodded thoughtfully but said nothing.

“Well, should we try opening this other door to see what happens?” David suggested.

"No better time than the present," was Tyler's reply.

They slowly opened the door. Powdery snow tumbled in and built up a small pile on the carpet. David realized they would have to shovel some of the snow inside the breezeway just to get out the door. How would they be able to do that without activating the automatic doors and causing more snow to blow inside?

"Tyler, do you know how to lock down the automatic doors so they won't open on us?" David asked.

Tyler looked up and studied the sides of the door frame.

"I think we could use a stick or a weight and it could jam the door. It might open an inch or two, but it wouldn't be able to slide all the way open."

"I'll go look for something that will work." David said and went back inside leaving Tyler to guard the door. Guarding the door from what specifically he could not say, but he felt better knowing Tyler was there.

Only five minutes had passed since the group split up, so David wasn't expecting any of the others to be back. He looked around the clothing section for something heavy and square that would work as a weight. They might also need some rope or wire to tie it in place. He wished he was downstairs in the tool section, but it was too far away.

Wandering around the quiet store was nerve wracking. The whole experience was getting more and more surreal. He could faintly hear Zoe and Miel across the store, and that made him feel a little bit better. Sears must not normally have any background music. He knew the electronics section would be humming with demo movies and loud stereo sound, but being on the second floor he could hear none of that. He walked around but found nothing useful. About to give up and tell Tyler he was going down stairs, he spotted a credit card receipt machine. He picked it up. It was heavy, the shape of a brick, and might just do the job.

He lifted it up and looked to see where the wires went. He could unplug both the computer connection and the power cord that was connected to a power strip underneath the counter. For a second, David hesitated. Receipt machines were likely to be costly items and not easy to replace. Would Sears be upset and make him pay for it? Then David burst out laughing, his voice echoing throughout the store. Who cares! There was thirty feet of snow piled up high outside. Sears wouldn't care if using their receipt machine helped save lives. He yanked the cord unceremoniously and stood up from behind the sales counter.

He looked up to see a white faced Miel and Zoe standing stock still, piled high with hats, scarves, gloves, and snowsuits. He wanted to laugh again, but refrained.

"You scared the heebie jeebies out of us!" Zoe cried. "We were walking along, alone we thought, when a maniacal laugh started echoing out of nowhere!" She then pelted David with a pair of gloves and hat. She was smiling now and visibly relieved. "Those are for you – you brat!" David smiled back hoping Miel was not too mad. She looked a little paler than Zoe.

"What's that for?" Zoe asked, pointing to his receipt machine as he pulled on the hat and gloves.

"Tyler and I are trying to find a way to block the automatic doors from opening so we can store some snow in the causeway. We were hoping something like this might work."

"The automatic doors also have locks you know. Some older models can be locked using the deadbolt. You don't even need store keys," Miel said. David was staring at her. How the heck did she know these things? Miel seemed to notice his incredulity. "Hey, I just pay attention," she responded.

Zoe jumped into the conversation. "And if the doors need keys we might be able to find a pair at one of the check-out stands. Usually managers lock and unlock the doors. My Aunt Chelsea once had a department store job and she had to lock up. She also spent most of the day at the front desk. You never know…"

"Well, let's just see if this will jam doors," David looked tiredly toward the exit.

David and the girls all jumped half a mile as a loud motor-like sound echoed through the large building.

"What the heck was that?" Miel asked. Zoe was picking up a handful of gloves she had dropped at the loud sound.

"I sure hope those guys are staying out of trouble," David said guessing the source of the sound. He was used to his friends causing trouble with noisy motors. It seemed to upset the girls but he shrugged and walked toward Tyler and the door. What did they expect him to do? Unless the sound started again or the guys didn't show up in five minutes, he was not going to worry about it.

"Hey Tyler, I found this heavy block…" David started his sentence and then paused. Tyler had took several clothing poles apart and wedged them on both sides of the automatic door to keep it from opening. Tyler was a genius! And he was quick. David mentally upgraded him in his mind. Tyler might be a little weird, but he was resourceful.

"Nice work Tyler!" he said.

"I can't seem to permanently lock the doors or shut off the automatic function yet, but this should work." Tyler paused to scrutinize his handiwork and continued, "As long as we don't spend too much time dancing on the automatic sensors." He smiled as he did exactly that, demonstrating just how strong his door jams were. He grabbed the receipt machine out of David's hands and added it to the top of the frame. "There, that should make it complete," Tyler added in a form of compliment nodding his head in satisfaction while looking to David for approval. David returned the nod.

He had almost forgot to tell Miel and Zoe the good news as they could not yet see the snow level outside.

"Check this out Miel, Zoe. There is a roof over the skywalk leading out to the parking garage. The snow is much lower than we expected. There is almost a clear path all the way out to the parking garage." David was exaggerating a bit. The path still had at least one feet of snow minimum. But still, it was better than they had expected. David failed to mention Tyler's observation that they still would not know what to do once they dug out to the parking lot.

All four of them went outside to check the weather conditions. Miel and Zoe decked themselves out in hats, scarves, and gloves. Tyler searched through the pile of winter wear and did the same before stepping outside.

It was good that they were bundled up because it was still quite cold and the wind was howling. The light from inside Sears reached about ten to fifteen feet out into the darkness. They could see large flakes of snow falling swiftly.

"Will it ever stop?" Miel wondered aloud.

"Or will it just keep falling until it buries us, like it seems to have buried the rest of the town?" Zoe asked none too ominously.

"Nah, the likelihood of that…" David started to say and then stopped when he realized how ridiculous he sounded and how ridiculous this whole situation was. Earlier he would have figured it was a dream, but he already went through the sequence of actions he always used to wake himself up from bad dreams. None of them had worked. If this was a dream, it was a realistic one.

"Shouldn't the boys be back with the shovels?" Miel asked.

"I was thinking the same thing," agreed Tyler.

The four walked back into the building in silence. Their general mood seemed to be swinging from silly, to dumbstruck, to afraid, to confused all within a ten minute period. David felt as though he had downed five Mountain Dews all at once. He had actually done that once with Cody when they were hanging out by the river last summer. All that caffeine had given him an uncomfortable jittery feeling, the exact same way he felt now, without drinking a single drink.

Their timing was perfect. The guys were approaching them single file. Cody came first pushing a large machine covered in layers of extension cords. Tanner was right behind him hidden in a pile of shovels, and Luke came last carrying two buckets that appeared to be heavily laden with odds and ends.

Cody was smiling like he had just saved the world.

"Check it out guys! Who needs to shovel when we have a snow blower!" Cody exclaimed.

David and Tyler looked closely at the big machine, obviously impressed with Cody's find. Miel and Zoe gathered round as well, although it was hard to tell if they spent more time looking at Cody or the snow blower.

"Nice work," said David. First impressed with Tyler's work on the automatic doors, he was equally impressed with Cody's quick thinking. This snow blower might make the time difference they needed. David wondered how high the machine would throw the snow, as he had never actually used one himself.

"Thanks for getting the hats," Luke told the girls. He started rifling through a few of them and modeled a funny one for Tanner.

"The most practical ones will probably be the ski masks and wool scarves. We also brought some snow pants and complete snow outfits. It just depends how much time we spend outside and how cold it gets," said Miel with a pause, "Does anyone know exactly HOW cold it is outside."

"Funny you should ask!" Luke explained and held up high the buckets he carried, proudly holding up a large outside thermometer. Ripping open the package, he pulled out the thermometer and headed toward the door.

"You are going to love what you see out there, Luke! We actually have a chance to dig out. Be careful not to stand in front of the automatic door sensors. We have the door jammed but we don't want to press our luck!" David called out as Luke headed outside to check the temperature. Zoe began poking through the buckets Luke had brought with him.

The whole group started working without any prompting. The relief and the excitement of the boys coming upstairs had now been replaced with a sense of urgency. The snow was falling fast and they needed to find a way out. No one other than Tyler and David had spoken about how futile their mission was. David doubted the reality of their predicament had slipped by Miel and he wondered why she had not spoken up yet. People did funny things when they were in groups. Or, David smiled, when they were around cute boys. He knew all the girls thought Cody was cute. Even smart, sensible girls like Miel.

"Miel, why don't you help Cody hook up these extension cords?" he asked.

Miel nodded in agreement and started ripping off the cardboard packaging for each cord then laying them side by side next to the snow blower.

Tyler joined Zoe in sifting through Luke's buckets and Tanner joined Luke outside to take a look. David decided to go outside as he contemplated how they should tackle this problem.

It was cold and quiet as he stepped out into the snow. His tennis shoes quickly got wet after having warmed up inside and he wished they had time to get snow boots. Maybe later if they kept on working.

Tanner and Luke were still pretty pumped up about their mission. He could tell they were talking excitedly about what to do next.

"We can start by using the snow blower to clear a path through the middle here. There is only a foot of snow in the center and we can widen it another foot at least," said Luke.

"Our trouble is going to be the wall of snow once we make it past the covered walkway. Even if we start to clear that space with shovels and buckets, we are going to have to put the snow someplace. And the only place to put the snow is up on the sides of the walkway. The snow is so high we can't even throw the snow over and down." Tanner added.

It was then that David thought he could see the look of realization on all of their faces. They were completing a fool's errand. Even if they dug through several feet of snow what would be the point? No one said anything.

"I was wondering if we might be able to walk on top of the snow?" David suggested, and he reached out and picked up a handful. It was light and airy, there was no chance it would hold his weight. He shrugged, "Well, maybe tomorrow it will freeze over and form a crust thick enough to walk on," but his voice held little confidence.

"You think we will be here overnight?" Tanner asked, as if taking the idea seriously for the first time.

"Maybe," David shrugged again and then went on, "I think we should only spend twenty minutes or so digging before we return to the theater. I don't want them to worry about us, and maybe they have found another way out."

Luke and Tanner nodded. Tanner pulled out his cell phone and checked for service. Luke followed suit and did the same thing with his phone.

"Still no service." Tanner confirmed. "So strange…what the heck could have happened?"

Feeling a little defeated the three boys went back inside. Tyler and Zoe had been unpacking and putting batteries in a variety of the headlamps and flashlights Luke had picked out from the hardware department. He had also managed to get a big floodlight, but had forgotten to get an additional extension cords to power it. They would probably need all the extension cords they brought in order to get the snow blower outside. Everyone grabbed a headlamp and shovel except Cody, who was slowly inching the snow blower toward the door. It was going to be a tight fit. Miel followed closely behind him as she let out the extension cord loop by loop.

The group headed out ahead of Cody and Miel. Zoe brought several flashlights which she put in the snow along the walkway for light. Spaced evenly they gave the area a magical glow. They approached the end of the walkway and stared at the mountainous wall of snow facing them. It was much taller than they had expected.

"Well, I guess we just start digging, eh?" David asked. He could tell everyone was nodding in agreement as their headlamps wavered up and down in the snow in front of them. They got to work, hesitantly at first, then more confidently as they understood how much snow they could shovel comfortably, as well as working in a formation that made sense. It became obvious that after the initial digging they would have to find a way to carry and deposit the extra snow to the sides and behind them.

"Vroom!" the loud sound of the snow blower caught them all of guard, some for the second time that night. Cody started up the snow blower and was beginning to widen the path between them and the Sears doors. Even though David could not see the smile on Cody's face, he imagined the bright grin he was wearing behind that ski mask. Cody loved machines and especially those that made annoyingly loud sounds.

David turned back and concentrated on the task at hand. It was frustrating work. Although they were making some progress on the snow between the store and the parking garage, they had not even hit the five foot tall wall of snow at the end of the path. That was going to take time! In addition, snow was still falling down and quickly replacing what they had already shoveled. It was not impossible work, but twenty minutes already passed and they would need to make a decision about going back to tell the other students waiting at the movie theater.

David stuck his shovel in the snow and looked back at Cody and the snow blower. Well, two of his questions were now answered. Yes, the snow blower could send snow a good six or seven feet in the air. But the answer to his second question – could the snow blower be useful in making a path through the walkway – was somewhat less promising. The blown snow was being thrown just high enough to hit the edge of the roof and making a nice steep pile on one side of the walkway. It would still work, but just not as effectively as David hoped.

Lost in thought, he hadn't noticed that everyone else had stopped shoveling except for Tyler. David briefly wondered why Tyler was working so hard, as he had been the first to recognize the futility of what they were doing.

"We need to check-in with the rest of the group. They may have found another way out or they might be worried about us," suggested David.

"Could we keep working and just send a few people back?" asked Zoe. When no one replied, David spoke softly.

"With it being so dark and the snow still falling, I don't know how much progress we will be able to make. Let's stick together as a group and rejoin the others. Then we can decide if we need to keep working tonight."

All of them agreed in silence. The hard work was causing them to breathe faster, each person sending out large puffs of foggy air. They slowly walked toward Cody and Miel. Cody had made it about halfway along the walkway with his snow blower and Miel was tidying up the path behind him with her shovel. As they approached David waved at Cody to shut down the snow blower.

"What's going on?" Cody asked, yelling as though the snow blower was still on.

"We are going to check in with the rest of the group. We may need to wait until tomorrow morning to start working again," David replied.

Cody looked a little confused. It was obvious he had been enjoying his part in the project. He shrugged and started backing the snow blower up to the building.

"Can we just leave it outside?" asked Miel.

"Nah…" Luke replied and then peered closely at the thermostat he had hung outside then continued, "The temperature is holding steady at about 30 degrees, so it could be alright, but we need to play it safe. If it gets really cold tonight it could damage the snow blower."

Miel laughed, "But there must be another twenty snow blowers downstairs right?"

Luke looked upset at first, but then changed his mind and smiled. "Yeah! You're right. Well, all the same we should bring it inside so it doesn't get frozen or buried."

It only took a few minutes to get all of their tools organized and put away. Half of them took off their hats and scarves but a few decided to keep them on. David decided to keep his hat and gloves with him. It was quite warm in the mall, but he wanted to keep them all the same, sort of like a security blanket.

David was the last inside. As he shut the door behind him a few large snowflakes floated inside - like they belonged there.

CHAPTER 5
THE MOVIES

Brittany was fuming mad. The entire field trip started out so well, and then it had gone down the toilet in a matter of hours. She and Cody hung out the entire morning. Brittany had always liked Cody, as did every other girl in class, but she knew that she was different from other girls and that somehow she was more deserving of Cody.

There were many reasons she was more deserving. She had never told anyone, especially not her best friend Molly, about how she spent summers working at the same resort restaurant her mother worked at. Ever since she was ten Brittany had washed dishes in the back of Red Beach Resort's restaurant. She worked over six hours a day, three hours at lunch and three at night. The owner had always kept her tucked in the back, even now that she was old enough to be legally working. Doing the dishes was disgusting work but she made thirty dollars a day and didn't have to pay taxes.

Working kept her out of her mother's hair and out of trouble at the resort over the summer. That was probably the only reason the resort owner had agreed to let her work at such a young age. Brittany would always save up all of her hard earned money so that she could buy the best clothes possible for school each fall. Whatever she could not afford her mother would buy for her. Recently they had even bought a new iPhone for Brittany. She looked haughtily around at the students from Mrs. Schmidt's class. Very few of them understood hard work and very few put as much time as she did into keeping up her image.

Of all the girls here she deserved Cody more than anyone else. She didn't mean to be snotty, but she considered herself better than most people and she wasn't afraid to say it. Some of the girls didn't even shave their legs or brush their teeth on a daily basis! She couldn't believe that they had all the privileges in the world and they still couldn't get simple hygiene down. Ewww!

Even though Cody spent most of his time hanging out with her and Molly in the morning, he had dropped them like hot potatoes once they got to the mall. She was not even sure what to make of Cody throwing popcorn at her when Miss Schmidt left. Was he doing it because he liked her or just to be a jerk? He was so difficult to read. Most guys would only tease you like that if they were interested, but Cody's smile when the oily popcorn hit her new shirt had been pretty gleeful. Like he knew exactly how upset he was making her.

Looking down at the oily stains on her shirt Brittany grimaced. They were not very noticeable, but a popcorn oil stain was not likely to come out in the wash very easily, if at all. The shirt had cost over forty dollars on sale, didn't Cody think about things like that? It always annoyed Brittany when her classmates, who never wore anything fashionable, would be careless about her clothes. This was not the first time someone has thoughtlessly ruined what she was wearing.

But then…nobody knew how hard she worked for what she owned. One day, when she graduated and moved to a big city, people would appreciate how much time and energy went into her appearance. For now, she would just have to deal with their lack of sophistication.

None of this changed that fact that she wanted Cody to be her boyfriend very badly! One way or another she was going to get what she wanted.

Actually this really weird situation might work toward her advantage, if they did not end up dead. Why hadn't anyone else been as upset as she was at their predicament? Everyone seemed to LOOK scared but not a single other person had really spoken up other than herself. And she had been shushed! Sheesh. Her classmates were either dimwitted or just weird. Brittany shivered at the thought of being stuck in a mall with a bunch of stupid people.

Well, at least Cody was among them. She couldn't even really count Molly or Lindsey. Lindsey was just a follower who never thought for herself and honestly, if she was being honest here, her best friend Molly was just plain stupid. Both at school and in life in general, it was only Molly's good fashion sense and knack at lying that compelled Brittany to continue their friendship. Molly could lie their way out of the tightest situation.

Brittany decided to stay with the main group waiting at the movie theater when Malachi and David led their small groups to separate ends of the mall. At first Brittany panicked. I mean, who wouldn't be freaking out if they walked outside of a movie to find the mall empty and a million feet of snow piled up high outside. Then things got even more freaky when not a single one of their cell phones had service.

The last straw was when Brittany saw the empty and abandoned food court. The chairs were scattered as if everyone had jumped up hastily and ran away, and it also appeared as though not a single person had taken their food with them. It was just plain weird. She knew about fat Americans, and if there was one thing a fat American would do in an emergency, it would be to take their fast food with them.

She laughed to herself for a minute at the mental picture that brought to mind. She could just see hundreds of shoppers grabbing their cafeteria trays, paper bags, and big forty-ounce sodas as they raced for the nearest exit. Then her laugh turned into a frown. That had not been the case. It seemed that every single meal and drink had been left behind in the rush to abandon the mall. What the heck could have caused so much alarm? Brittany wondered briefly if the food might be bad, or releasing some kind of poison gas. She doubted it, but she would not be the first one to try the leftover food.

The image of big, greasy, fat Americans running for their lives with their arms full of food gave Brittany a nice image for contrast. She looked down at her slim figure and admired her tiny arms and calves.

In addition to looking fashionable Brittany and her Mom had always prided themselves on staying thin. They stocked up on Weight Watchers frozen meals, Slimfast milkshakes, and their favorite fruits and diet colas. Brittany would read about the diets famous models were using and try them herself. She had been on the popcorn diet, the rice diet, and the cucumber diet just to name a few.

Brittany never had much time for exercise but she still managed to fit in a few aerobic workouts from time to time. She shunned sweaty school sports.

Even in middle school she had always brought her own lunch to school. One Slimfast shake and a banana - everyday. She always ate with Molly in the Annex so that none of the teachers or other students could keep track of what she ate. Sometimes she would go into the main cafeteria and was absolutely horrified at what everyone else was eating. Fried burritos, tater tots, cookies, and chocolate milk. As far as Brittany was concerned, the girls in her class who were overweight deserved it - they had no self control.

Brittany rubbed her forehead to erase the frown wrinkles. She had been toggling back and forth between her game and phone pad on her iPhone as she checked for service. So far there had been nothing. What the heck would make cell phones and satellites disappear all at once? Snow wouldn't do that. And most cell phones like her iPhone relied on satellites, right? She wasn't sure of the answer and wished she could get on the internet and Google the answer.

Hmmph! Sitting here bored, she now wished she had gone with

Malachi or David. She thought their best bet for a rescue would be to stick together and she was so sure that cell phone service would reconnect soon, or some group of Navy Seals would come swooping down in helicopters to save them. I mean, if Miss Schmidt had made it out alive wouldn't she have been telling everyone about the lost school children? And didn't governments and local police always make it a priority to save kids, the elderly, and pets - in that order? For a second she thought that maybe the Americans didn't give a hoot about Canadians, but then she remembered that Americans thought Canadians were like long lost cousins.

She really wanted to go with Cody's group, but then Miel and Zoe had decided to go and Brittany hated being around Zoe. Zoe always confronted Brittany when she was trying to have fun or get her own way. Most people were scared of Brittany when she was trying to get what she wanted and would back down immediately.

Brittany did not intentionally mean to be a bully, but her mother had taught her at an early age that if she didn't stand up for herself no one would. As Brittany perfected her ability to demand what she wanted, she noticed that other people were intimidated by her. Like they thought there was some special unspoken rule about being polite. Brittany was never one to be polite in order to let others walk all over her. If people cared more about politeness they could be the last in line. Every time someone backed down to her demands, Brittany felt powerful, but she also despised people after they gave in to her. That was the problem with her whole class. As she looked around briefly at the students milling around, she couldn't identify a single one who had even the tiniest bit of gumption.

Molly, who had also been playing games on her iPhone, tapped Brittany on the shoulder.

"You got any cell phone service yet?" asked Molly.

Brittany looked at her with a scathing glance. Can you get any stupider? Brittany thought. If I had service I would not be sitting here playing games, I would be screaming and calling my Mom! But Brittany refrained from telling Molly what she was really thinking.

Molly could be awfully sensitive sometimes and she couldn't alienate her best friend right now.

"No," was her simple reply. She ignored Molly and went back to her game.

Right in the middle of trying to finish a level in Monument Valley an ugly thought crept into Brittany's mind. What if Miss Schmidt never made it out of the movie theater? What if her rotting body was still in the bathroom or in the last row? Then there would be no one to tell the Navy Seals that a class of thirty students had been left behind in the mall. Ewww! Brittany knew that she watched too many horror movies for her age - it was her mother's favorite pastime - but she could not help freaking herself out. And if she was going to be freaked out so should other people.

"Guys! What if Miss Schmidt was left for dead back in the movie theater? Then no one will ever know that we were abandoned in the mall!" It did not take much to raise Brittany's voice to a shriek and most of her classmates heard her loud and clear.

It was quiet for a moment and then someone spoke up. "Even if Miss Schmidt is laying dead somewhere back there, the other chaperones would have made it out." Brittany looked around to see who had shot down her idea, but couldn't tell who it was. Why were people so scared to speak up. Wimps.

"Even so, you wouldn't want to be responsible for leaving Miss Schmidt gasping for breath because we were too lazy to look for her?" Brittany replied. She was annoyed. She had failed to see that flaw in her thinking. But she was also pleased about that last little touch… "gasping for breath." Maybe she should write screen plays for horror scripts some day. Better yet, she should be an actress in a scary movie.

"I looked in the movie theater and Zoe checked the bathrooms." Victoria spoke up and moved toward Brittany. Her tone was not defiant or weak. "But I think Brittany is on to something. I didn't actually check the floor between each row, and I doubt Zoe checked every stall. We would be pretty stupid not to do a thorough search of the movie theater. Even if someone comes to save us in the next hour or so we would want to make sure there were no survivors left behind."

Victoria didn't usually talk very much. Brittany was glad for the support, even if it did come from a quiet loner like Victoria.

"We will probably still be sitting here for another half hour before everyone gets back from Macy's and Sears. We might as well search the theater." Brittany said.

People started volunteering to search different wings of the theater. There were twelve different theaters in all, and four bathrooms to search. Victoria offered to stay in place at the front of the theater in case anyone returned and wondered where they were. They agreed to search in pairs and return in ten or fifteen minutes at the most. Brittany could tell that Victoria was keeping a mental note of everything. Even if Victoria did not speak up much, Brittany knew that the girl didn't miss a beat. She seemed to have ears that heard everything. When Brittany was gossiping with Molly in class she always did a quick head check to make sure Victoria wasn't listening.

Brittany volunteered Lindsey and Molly to go with her to the far corner of the theater. They were going to search the wing with the R rated movies. The theater had loosely organized their films so that most of the rated R films were shown in the south wing while most of the G, PG, and PG-13 films were shown in the east wing. Brittany suspected they made that arrangement to keep kids from buying tickets to a PG movie and sneaking into an R rated movie. Brittany had only done that once with Molly when they had wanted to see the newest M. Night Shayamalan flick. Most of the time her mother would take her to rated R movies or rent them to watch at home.

Brittany walked in the middle with Lindsey on her right and Molly on her left. She was always naturally the center of the pack. Another group of boys were searching the first four theaters in the same wing while Brittany and her friends were going to search the back four and the women's restroom.

Molly started heading toward the restroom but Brittany grabbed her arm. "Let's search the movie theaters first, then we can check the bathroom at the end." Molly did not protest and let Brittany lead her down the dark corridor. As they left the sound and lights of the front part of the movie house it got appropriately spooky. Brittany shivered in delight. As long as she could forget why they were still stuck in the mall she could have a good time scaring her friends.

She grabbed Lindsey's arm and deliberately slowed their pace. There were electronic signs blinking the name of each film in red. Brittany quickly scanned the four titles, a movie called "Insidious: Chapter 4" was playing in the first theater. Brittany remembered seeing the movie trailer a month or two ago, and the trailer looked scary.

"Let's check this one first," Brittany ordered. She could feel Lindsey pulling back from her as she dragged her two friends into the theater.

Everything was dark at first and then they were blasted by a loud screeching and bright light. All three girls jumped back and screamed, but their exit was blocked by the door swinging behind them. Brittany let out a stifled "eep!" but then laughed. They had walked into the theater right in the middle of a particularly scary part of the movie. Brittany could feel Molly and Lindsey shaking right along with her as they crept forward into the theater. This was one of the reasons she loved scary movies!

The next part of the movie was quiet. A young man was carrying a small boy through a dark house. She shivered and then grabbed Molly and Lindsey's arms with a tighter grip. No more looking at the screen, she was properly scared now.

The hallway brought them right into the middle of the room. There were four rows of seats in front of them and about twenty rows to the back. They turned as one to stare up at the seats above them. Back in the mall it had seemed like such a simple and logical task, to check each movie theater thoroughly for any people. Now that there were just three of them in a dark theater with horror movie sounds all around them, well, it just didn't seem like a good idea any more. Brittany knew they needed to get through this, so she pulled Lindsey and Molly by the arms and started up the stairs. Thank goodness she was in the middle!

They walked slowly up the stairs, looking down each row for signs of hidden people but all they saw were a few abandoned popcorn bags and sodas. The smell of popcorn was still strong, but slightly stale. When they reached the highest row they peered down in anticipation, but saw nothing. They let out a collective sigh of relief, and slowly turned back. Brittany dreaded having to look back at the movie screen. Luckily, the movie had moved on to a more benign scene. Although the music was now a lighter tune, it was that kind of cheery horror film music that still implied something bad might happen anytime soon.

"OK, I think we checked those rows well enough. Let's run down and check the rows in front and then get out of here!" Brittany said in a voice that sounded much more confident that she really felt.

"Sounds good to me," agreed Molly.

They ran down the stairs quickly, but still held one another's arms with a tight grip. When they reached the bottom and confirmed every row empty, Brittany dropped their arms and ran shrieking from the theater. She was not really that scared, she just loved the adrenaline rush. Sure enough, she had scared Molly and Lindsey to their wits end and they came screaming after her. Right on cue the horror film soundtrack started to kick in high gear. Molly slammed the door behind them with a solid thud and they stopped to catch their breath.

"You are such a brat, Brittany!" Lindsey complained. Even if Lindsey did follow Brittany around like a puppy, she could tell when Brittany was purposely teasing to get her upset.

"I am so scared! Do we really have to finish checking the other theaters?" Molly's words were hard to comprehend through her labored breathing. She was shaking and twisting her hands together.

Brittany took a moment to finish catching her breath then replied. "We have to finish what we started. But look, the last three theaters don't have horror films. They won't be so scary." Brittany linked arms with her two friends and pulled them along to the next theaters.

The second theater appeared to be more abandoned with pop corn boxes and sodas in the seats. Taking a swift count Brittany estimated that there had been at least thirty people watching this show. Where had they all gone?

In the last theater they were comfortable enough to quit holding on to one another. The girls split up so they could check the rows more quickly. As Brittany was approaching the last row Molly gave a terrified squeak across the room that caused Brittany to jump.

"What is it?" Brittany asked quietly across the room. The movie suddenly ended and they were plunged into darkness.

"I think I see a body on the floor," came Molly's wavering voice from across the room. Brittany was not sure what to do next. It was obvious that Molly wasn't going to get any closer to the body and she sure as heck wasn't counting on Lindsey, who had already taken two steps down behind Molly. It was going to be up to Brittany to get a closer look.

Brittany started to make her way to the girls, but going down a dark row was not appealing to her. She decided to run back down and around the well lit main aisle.

"Where are you going?" shrieked Molly, no longer trying to be quiet.

"I'm coming. I'm coming, don't freak out!" Brittany snapped back. Molly was useless under pressure. Brittany supposed that all the years she and her mom had watched horror films gave her the guts to deal with real life horror.

Just as Brittany had almost reached Molly and Lindsey, the theater lights came on to indicate the end of the movie credits. With the extra light Molly could clearly see what she had been looking at.

"Oh…I see. It was just a jacket," Molly whispered. Still, Molly did not move any closer to the jacket, or dead body, or whatever she was looking at.

Brittany rudely pushed Molly out of the way to get a better look, and Molly did not seem to mind. Now Brittany could see why Molly thought she had seen a dead body. The large leather trench coat had been hooked partially on the side arm of the chair and looked like a person slumped in the chair. Brittany gave the coat a good kick just to make sure there was nothing hidden underneath. Sure enough, it collapsed into a heap on the floor. Brittany picked the coat up and swung it around to show Molly.

"See, it's just a coat," Brittany laughed, but when she saw Molly start to cry she changed her tone. "But I know what you mean Molly. In the dark it really did look like a slumped over body. I would have been freaked out too."

Brittany turned the coat and looked at it more closely. It was the first evidence of people they had found except for discarded food. She started reaching inside the pockets to look for clues about the owner of the coat.

"Are you going to steal from the coat?" Lindsey asked.

"No," Brittany glared back. "I'm just trying to find out who left this coat here. This is the first piece of evidence - besides popcorn bags - that real people were here a few hours ago." She kept on looking, and remembered that trench coats usually had hidden pockets. "With it being so cold outside I am surprised that anyone would have left their coat. Even if it really was a major emergency, maybe this guy was in the bathroom when they were evacuating the mall."

Score! Brittany reached into the hidden pocket and her hand grabbed what must have been a leather wallet. She pulled it out and opened it up for all to see. It was a pretty basic wallet, not too thick or thin. Instinctively she opened the inside of the wallet first to look for cash. She counted a little under twenty dollars worth of small bills. Next, she pulled out his cards and identification. His name was Brandon Miller, age twenty and he lived at W. 310 Mallon. In the wallet he kept one debit card, several espresso punch cards, and a GameStop membership.

"Well, this doesn't really tell us that much. All the same, we should bring this coat and wallet with us." said Brittany.

All of a sudden the coat gave out a loud buzz and vibration. They all jumped, but Brittany the most since she was holding the coat. The familiar buzz continued and Brittany gave a sigh of relief. She realized there must be a phone inside the coat. It might even be ringing! Which would mean they had cell phone service! Undaunted, Brittany thrust her hand into the hidden pocket without a second thought. If she could get phone service…she would be a hero.

Sure enough, Brandon's coat was hiding a vibrating phone. She pulled it out to discover an older cell phone. Hoping beyond hope, Brittany opened the phone without looking at the screen and put it up to her ear."Hello," she asked tentatively. There was no response but the phone continued to buzz loudly in her ear. She looked down at the screen and saw a repeating phrase next to a small ringing bell icon. "It is just an alarm," she said out loud in disappointment. She checked the phone just in case, but there were no bars indicating cell service.

By this time, Brittany recognized that even her nerves were shaken. They needed to finish up their search and return to the group

"Let's get going," she suggested.

"I agree!" said Molly enthusiastically. The three of them headed down the stairs. Right before heading out to the hallway Lindsey fell momentarily behind. Brittany noticed and called back to her.

"C'mon Lindsey, let's go."

"I'm coming," Lindsey replied, but not before Brittany had noticed that Lindsey had been staring intently at the movie projection box high above the seats. It was just starting to roll advertisements as it prepared for the next show. Brittany would have to ask Lindsey exactly what she was thinking – but not now. Right now they just needed to get back to civilization.

CHAPTER SIX
SEARCH PARTIES

Malachi, Micah, Nolan, and Madison walked back into the main theater holding their Radio Shack bags. Micah dreaded the return at first. He had this sinking feeling that everyone had disappeared or been rescued while they were searching Macy's. Micah was generally very logical, but part of the curse of being logical was that he kept inventory of all the different possibilities and outcomes. Even though he knew statistically which outcomes were more likely, it did not always prevent him from contemplating the less likely ones. Now that everyone had disappeared from the mall, statistical analysis was becoming particularly difficult, throwing his sense of confidence out the window. Under the present circumstances he had a hard time discounting any possibility.

So as the foursome approached the theater and he didn't see a single student milling in the hall, he thought one of his predictions - rescue, escape, or disappearance – might be true. Of all the people to get stuck with alone in the mall, Malachi and Nolan would be last on his list.

His blood pressure spiked slightly as they approached the theater and not a soul was in sight. Then Victoria stepped out of the theater to greet them and he relaxed a bit. As soon as she told them what was going on, Micah's heart rate returned to normal. They were still in a predicament, but at least they were in it together. He wished he had gone with David's group instead.

"We grabbed these Walkie Talkies from Radio Shack. Now we can move around and stay in contact without worrying about losing anyone. Micah also snagged a bunch of flashlights and batteries in case the electricity goes out." Nolan announced, while he tried to open the hard plastic packaging around the Walkie Talkies. Malachi looked at him, slightly disgusted, and then pulled out an old Swiss Army Knife and handed it to Nolan.

"Thanks," Nolan said, glancing up briefly at Malachi.

What the heck was Malachi doing with a knife? Micah wondered. He noted the information for later contemplation. Malachi obviously had experience with knives and no respect for school authority. Micah guessed that it was lucky Malachi hadn't been searched for weapons at the border crossing. Micah didn't know for sure that knives were illegal to bring to the U.S., but he did know that customs was usually picky about declaring such items. Regardless, utility knives were banned from school so Malachi should have never had one in the first place. There was much Micah didn't understand about Malachi.

"Madison, would you help me unpack the batteries and flashlights?" Micah asked politely. They might as well get everything in working order before the lights went out. Micah considered losing electricity to be another inevitable consequence of the snow storm. The power lines to the mall might be underground, but such heavy snowfall was likely to interrupt service at some point. He wondered briefly if the mall had any backup generators.

Malachi's knife came in quite handy during the next few minutes as the small group tore into thick plastic packaging. Victoria and Bailey jumped in to help unpack the flashlights. Malachi however, seemed to have no interest in the work and began to wander back toward the concession stands. Before getting too far Malachi turned around and glared at the group.

"Make sure you return the knife to me when you are finished," he abruptly said, then added in a less threatening voice, "It was a gift from my dad and I don't want to lose it."

Micah added that information to his databank on Malachi as well. Malachi's dad wasn't around much if you believed the gossip heard around town. Ah well, piecing family life together was not one of Micah's strong suits, but he just couldn't leave any detail uncategorized, no matter how irrelevant or odd.

Micah grabbed almost all the batteries he could find at Radio Shack. He mentally counted the packages, there were thirty-five total. He wasn't sure where else in the mall they could find batteries in a pinch. He knew Sears would have flashlights in the tools section, but not necessarily batteries.

He paused from his work unwrapping the batteries to look up for a minute. Sure enough, there was a mall map and directory across from the escalator. He would like to have a closer look when they were done preparing the flashlights.

It didn't take very long for their small group to unwrap what they needed. Most of the flashlights Micah had found at Radio Shack were small, so they only required AAA batteries. He left all of the AA batteries in their packaging for later use. The Walkie Talkies also needed AAAs. As Victoria finished putting the last of the batteries into the flashlights Madison was lining up the flashlights into groups of five. A quick count and Micah realized they had twenty-two flashlights. Not a bad start for when the lights went out.

"Let's each take a flashlight and distribute them to the other students when they come back. Some people will have to share, so if you know friends that will want to stick together we should ask them to take one or two per group," Micah suggested. Madison was busy throwing away the packaging while Victoria was handing out flashlights. She was even sweet enough to track Malachi down and pointedly give him his knife back, along with a flashlight. Malachi had been hunting and pecking around the concessions stand. Micah watched him munch on a few handfuls of popcorn and check out the hot dog warmer.

Nolan, Victoria and Bailey were reading the directions that came with the Walkie Talkies. The other students were so engrossed with the 'Walkie Talkies,' that Micah took the opportunity to walk over and examine the store map.

Micah had only been to Northtown Mall once in his life, and therefore he felt uncomfortable with the lack of knowledge about his surroundings. He did not have a photographic memory, but he did a good job of organizing information spatially.

First he took the time to get to know the basic shape of the mall. It was designed as a two level rectangle, much like a figure eight. In the center of the mall was the food court on the second level, more snacks on the first level, and a small basement in the middle housed a video arcade and pizza shop. While the majority of the food was centrally located in the middle of the mall there were still a few places, like Mrs. Field's, Orange Julius, and Cinnabon on the perimeter. The southwest corner held the movie theater on the second floor and Barnes and Noble on the first floor. The northwest corner was anchored by Macy's, J.C. Penny on the northeast, Nordstrom in the east, and Sears on the southeast corner. There was also a large REI store located on both levels near the north walkway.

He kept gathering the most pertinent facts. There were about two hundred stores in the mall. It was a pretty big mall for Spokane, which was really a mid-size city. There were only three exits leading directly out of the mall with another eight exits connecting to big department stores. Nothing on the map gave him information about the hidden tunnels and employee-only sections of the mall. He knew there were places where mall employees entered and garbage moved out, but these were not specified on the public mall map. He hoped that they would not be there long enough that they would have to explore those areas.

Logically Micah believed that within the next few days they would either be rescued or die from exposure once the heaters stopped working. He could not see any other scenario that would keep them locked up in the mall for longer than that. If he could help his classmates make it through the next few days they would live, in any of the good scenarios. The scenarios that ended badly seemed to be just as likely, but he tried not to spend too much time dwelling on those possibilities.

The noise level behind him seemed to be growing. He took a minute and looked over his shoulder. People were slowly returning to the main foyer after searching their section of the theater. He could hear a few snippets of conversation from where he was standing.

"There are not enough flashlights to go around, so some of us will need to share. Brittany, would you, Lindsey and Molly mind sharing two?" Victoria asked the girls.

"No, we each need our own flashlight. We may not be together the whole time so you will need to ask someone else to share," Brittany responded curtly. She grabbed three flashlights from the pile, ignoring the two Victoria was offering her, and started walking away. Victoria was left speechless at Brittany's rudeness. That girl could really be mean Micah thought and as he continued to listen he looked at the map.

"I hope it's ok that we are eating the popcorn," said Nolan as he stuffed a handful in his mouth.

"The popcorn would go bad eventually anyway silly!" Bailey assured him, "We probably shouldn't start eating the wrapped candy…unless we are here for more than twenty-four hours."

A choking sound interrupted Bailey's musings. "Ugh, I put too much butter on my popcorn. I didn't realize that was possible. Oh well, I'll just get a new one," said Molly as she spit a half chewed mouthful back into her bag.

Micah quickly calculated what was happening. Even though he could not see inside the theater he was one hundred percent positive that Malachi had started handing out popcorn buckets to everyone who wanted one. Well, Micah thought, Bailey was right about the popcorn spoiling if it was not eaten in the near future, and it was approaching dinnertime. Even his stomach was rumbling a bit.

Wait a minute. David and his group should have been back from Sears at least a half hour ago. Micah checked his watch. If they did not show up in the next ten to fifteen minutes they would have to send a search party out to look for them.

Micah reverted attention to the mall map. The next step for the class, if all the exits were blocked by snow, was to form search parties and check the mall for other survivors. It just seemed logical. If the mall was evacuated and they managed to miss an entire class of students in the movie theater, wouldn't they also miss a person here or there in the rest of the mall? To Micah it seemed highly likely that would be the case. In fact, he was slightly surprised that they had not seen any other people in the mall so far. They were a noisy bunch of kids and he was sure their voices were loud enough to draw attention to anyone within shouting distance. Still, if someone was on the opposite side of the mall they may not be able to hear them. So, the next step would be to search the mall thoroughly.

He wondered if the class had found anything interesting while searching the theater - probably not - Micah was sure he would have heard some commotion. The Walkie Talkies Nolan had picked out would make searching the mall easier. He wished that David had a Walkie Talkie right now to tell them what was happening at Sears.

Hmmm...what else would they need to accomplish tonight? Well, Malachi was right about one thing. They would need to eat. Popcorn was a start, but they might as well eat up the warm food in the theater and food court. The hot dogs Malachi had been eying would be a good start. They should also eat whatever else was sitting under the warming lights in the food court. Micah remembered seeing a whole counter of pizzas at Sabarro's and some burgers and tater tots sitting around behind the counters.

His mind drifting, he realized that they might need to check the food court for fire hazards. He wondered if any of that equipment would need to be turned off to keep it from overheating or burning. Probably not, but they might as well be safe and double check. Smiling, he realized that he was thinking of food because he was hungry. Getting a bite to eat might be one of their first priorities. He could just imagine how hungry some of his fellow teenage friends could be.

Micah had two more ideas. First, he might want to put Pierce in charge of organizing and going through the food and equipment. It was a little known fact that Pierce was actually a pretty decent cook and food aficionado. His parents owned a local gourmet restaurant in Canada and he had grown up around the stuff. Micah knew that Pierce wouldn't admit it to the other guys, but Micah ate at their restaurant often enough for Micah to notice Pierce playing around in the kitchen.

Secondly, almost as an afterthought, Micah realized it would probably be best for them to drink bottled water and sodas until they figured out what was going on. He remembered hearing something about not drinking water after a nuclear accident. While there had been no specific clue hinting at nuclear accident, better safe than sorry.

They had a decent supply of flashlights and Walkie Talkies to begin with, but if they searched the entire mall top to bottom they might as well score more flashlights from Sears. So whichever group was assigned to search that area should pick up flashlights. With two hundred stores total, each group could probably search one-sixth of the mall and then report back.

He would also have to organize some groups to search the bathroom and employee-only areas. That might be the trickiest part. Most of the employee-only entrances were locked with a keypad and it might be next to impossible to get the combination. Perhaps they had records in the mall's main office. He earlier noticed a sign pointing toward the mall office at the west entrance between here and Macy's. Maybe the information booth was near the mall office.

Wait a minute! It might be easy to enter the employee-only part of the mall through the back of different storefronts. Didn't most stores connect through a hallway in the back? He wasn't sure but that could make their search job just that much easier.

Next, they should check out the non-wireless internet options. So far, no one had cell phone service, and he was pretty darn sure his friends would be screaming at the top of his or her lungs if they were connecting to the outside world. Even if all the satellite and Wi-Fi connections had been terminated they still might be able to get access through a landline. The mall office or the Apple store seemed like a likely place. In fact the Apple store might be the first place to check.

Micah ran his finger along the list of stores. He found the electronics category and then BINGO, the Apple store was on the second level. Perfect! Someone would need to check that out immediately. Why hadn't he thought of it earlier?

So check the electronics, get some food, and search the mall. He only hoped that David and his companions would come back with good news about a possible escape route. Their lateness was beginning to bother Micah. They could only be late for a really good reason or a really bad reason. He hoped it was the former.

Micah took a few more minutes to look through the mall map for ideas. If they found no way to connect with the outside world, no way to escape, and no other people in the mall, then they would be forced with the reality of spending the night in the mall. Spending the night? Micah laughed to himself. It sounded ludicrous, but also like any kids fantasy, getting to shop all night long with a mall all to themselves. The only problem was they were not here to shop while their lives were at stake.

What to do if they did spend the night in the mall? Well, most of them were young enough to stay up all night without sleeping. But a few of them were bound to want to find a comfortable place to lay down. Besides, thought Micah practically, they would be a lot better equipped to deal with tomorrow's challenges after a good nights rest. Who knows what kind of escape or rescue opportunities might present themselves after the sun rose.

Bedding…he ran his finger down the categories of stores again. Under Specialty Store he found the Mattress Outlet. That would work perfectly! They must have at least twenty or so beds to choose from. He also smiled at the thought of who would fight for what bed or complain that they had to share a king size bed. There would probably be pillows at the mattress store but he couldn't remember if they sold blankets or comforters. It was getting a little chilly in the mall. He suspected that the mall heating system would drop the temperature of the mall a couple of degrees automatically at night to save money. They could find blankets at Macy's or JC Penny, and if the electricity went out they would be in an entirely different predicament.

Where would they find heat? They could make a fire, but how the heck would the smoke escape and what would they burn? He checked the list of stores again for a fireplace store. After going through the entire list once he checked the map yet again. Nothing! Well if worse came to worse they would have to burn wood in a makeshift fire pit and break a hole in the ceiling to let the smoke escape, unless the snow covered the entire mall roof as well. He instinctively looked up and then over at the height of the current snow level. It would take at least twenty more feet of snow to cover the roof.

Ridiculous! Of course, the current amount of snow was no less ridiculous. Micah shook his head. What a news story this would make if they make it out alive. But what he was starting to be was less and less sure of the prospects of that really happening.

Feeling confident that he had thought of ninety percent of the most important tasks to be accomplished, Micah made his way back to the theater to find out what had happened since he left. He would give himself five minutes to listen and gather information before sharing some of his ideas. Then five more minutes before he would suggest they send a search party to look for David and the others. In his entire life, Micah had never before crossed his fingers for good luck. There was a first time for everything he thought, as he crossed fingers on both hands.

CHAPTER 7
FOOD COURT

Pierce was tired and hungry. He and Ethan had just finished searching the movie theaters on the R-rated side. They did a thorough check of each theater and even spent extra time looking inside every bathroom stall. Pierce took this job seriously, and it infuriated him to see Brittany and her friends treating this situation with such giddiness. He and Ethan had followed them down the same hall minutes ago, only to watch Brittany drag her friends screaming and giggling down the hall.

He was tired and hungry for many reasons. The night before the field trip he had been helping his parents prepare for a big banquet at the restaurant. Usually he would be at the restaurant to help, but since the field trip was so important, he had done lots of prep work ahead of time instead. He had made 120 chocolate Nanaimo Bars that had to be chilled overnight. Pierce wished he could have brought them on the field trip to see how they tasted. His mom had saved several samples in the cooler, but by the time he got home, they would be less than perfect, and in cooking, perfection was key.

Pierce loved to cook but he never shared that part of his life with anyone at school. At home he watched dozens of cooking shows that he recorded on their DVR. One of his favorites was the old school Japanese "Iron Chef," the one they made before "Iron Chef America." He loved the original Japanese version the best. Sometimes when he was working with his parents in their family restaurant they would pretend to have their own competitions in the kitchen, even if they were just racing for the best time or presentation of their regular dishes.

Pierce was never paid anything to help out around the restaurant. His parents had always been food aficionados and opened their own gourmet restaurant when he was just three years old. Pierce had two sisters but none of the children were expected to help out.

Ironically each of them fell in love with a different aspect of the restaurant business. Alice, his oldest sister, helped design and decorate the main floor. She had a knack for style and helped her Mom change the décor every few years. His little sister, Amelia, had a passion for decadent pastries. She could bake the best éclairs, cakes, and cookies, or anything to do with chocolate for that matter. In fact she had just taught him how to make the Nanaimo bars he had been working on last night. Pierce on the other hand loved everything about the family business from the back kitchen to the front of the house.

Instead of getting paid, Pierce and his siblings had everything they wanted within reason. Their parents made it very clear that they were starting a college fund for each child, and if one of them wanted to take over the family business, that child would be required to go to college for four years and get a job somewhere else for at least two years before returning to the restaurant. There were times Pierce would argue with his parents about this stipulation, but they were dead set on the idea. They wanted each of their children to have a college education and get some real life experience before returning to their small town. His parents reminded him that whatever degree he earned, and no matter where he worked, he would be bringing back valuable experience.

Usually on school days Pierce would have a hard time concentrating on his school work as he thought about what was going on at the restaurant. (That was how much he loved food!) But during this field trip he had hardly thought about the restaurant.

Of course the field trip itself had been fascinating and now this strange predicament - whatever this weird situation was. He could hardly wrap his head around the idea that they were in an empty mall covered by thirty feet of snow. He kept waiting for someone to come running down the hall yelling "April Fools" or "You're on Candid Camera!" But instead, everything seemed eerily normal.

The movies were still rolling, music poured from several of the mall stores, and the smell of popcorn oozed out of the theater as it did every day. In those respects all was as it was supposed to be. The only problem was that wall of snow outside. Pierce hoped that David would come back from Sears with some good news.

All of a sudden he heard a new sound – a rhythmic pumping. Pierce looked up from the bench he was sitting on to see Malachi adding excessive pumps of fake butter to a king size popcorn. Pierce smiled. Wasn't it every kid's dream to have the concession stand worker put extra butter on their popcorn? Though he understood the difference between synthetic movie popcorn butter and freshly warmed organic butter, he still appreciated the former. He was a food aficionado – of all food – fast food included. Pierce's stomach rumbled so loud that Ethan heard.

"Gosh dude, you must be hungry," Ethan commented and then started patting his own stomach. "I would be hungry too but I already downed a king-sized popcorn during the movie. I might go for a hot dog, though." he added as an afterthought.

"I guess I am a little hungry," Pierce replied to Ethan. It had been about six hours since lunch and he had skipped the snacks during the movie. He watched Malachi hand the popcorn bag across the counter to Brittany and pretend to demand money. Malachi must be using the food as an opportunity to flirt with the girls. Well, if the girls were going to get free popcorn, Pierce might as well join them in line.

"Ethan, wanna get in line and order some food from Malachi?"

he asked.

Ethan looked over and smiled. "Sure," he replied.

They walked up and got in line behind Brittany, Molly, and Lindsey. Pierce noticed that Malachi seemed to be having a lot of fun playing the concession stand employee so he decided to heckle him a bit.

"The lines moving too slow. Hurry it up!" he called out in a gruff voice. Malachi looked upset for a second and glared at Pierce, but when he saw Pierce smile at him, he relaxed and shouted back.

"If you aren't satisfied with the service you can complain to my manager!"

"I will!" Pierce replied.

Brittany giggled and started to play the part. "We would like two large Cokes and a large Sprite, please," she said and then turned and asked the other girls what they wanted. "We would also like two Twizzlers, Junior Mints, and a Kit Kat."

Pierce had to laugh. Usually girls were all concerned about their weight and eating in front of guys. But in this situation it was like eating dinner. And, come to think about it, he supposed they all had bigger problems to worry about in the large scheme of things. Maybe Brittany was right in taking a lighthearted approach. He shouldn't be so serious about everything all the time. Laughter made the world a better place.

He did think it was a little weird that Lindsey and Molly always let Brittany boss them around. Why didn't they give Malachi their own order or join in on the fun? He could tell Lindsey was just shy in general, but Molly seemed to have no personality whatsoever. He glanced at Lindsey's wavy brown hair. She did have the prettiest brown eyes to match. Pierce shook his head. This was no time to renew his crush on Lindsey. He had always secretly had a thing for her, but he admitted he was even too shy to think about her – especially right now.

Malachi made a great show of getting the sodas and candy for the girls. He seemed to be relishing his role as a customer service guy.

Pierce watched him manage to overfill the cups with ice, pour it all out, and then overfill the cups again with soda. He found the right candy bars, added a few extra Kit Kats to the pile, and then promptly asked for two hundred dollars with a straight face. Brittany played her chosen role right back.

"Two hundred dollars! This theater is a rip-off!" Brittany shrieked in mock glee as she thrust the sticky sodas into her friends' hands, then gathered up the candy bars to stuff them into her own coat pockets.

The girls moved on without a glance as Pierce and Ethan moved forward to the snack counter.

"What'll it be?" asked Malachi in a jolly tone.

"One of each candy bar and a large Dr. Pepper." Ethan requested. Both Malachi and Pierce gave Ethan a quick double take.

"Every kind of candy?" Pierce asked. "But you don't even like Junior Mints!"

"C'mon, since when have I ever been able to get every kind of candy? This is a once in a lifetime chance. Besides, I am not going to eat all of it...just most of it!" Ethan replied with a wiry smile.

Pierce could not fault Ethan's logic. He looked over at Malachi who was gleefully fulfilling Ethan's order. Malachi grabbed a popcorn tub and started stuffing one of every candy choice into the tub. Pierce watched Malachi intently as he started on the bottom row of the cheapest candy and moved up to the most expensive. Ethan must have ordered hundred dollars worth of candy, Pierce mused.

Malachi finished up Ethan's order and then looked at Pierce expectantly. It took a minute for Pierce to catch on.

"Uh, yeah. Can you get me a Twix?" Pierce ordered.

"Nothing else? You want something to drink?" Malachi asked as if surprised Pierce was not ordering the same thing as Ethan.

"Nah, I'll just eat from Ethan's stash." Pierce responded.

"This is my candy, you can get your own," was Ethan's quickly reply. With that comment, Ethan wrapped his arms protectively around his candy filled popcorn tub and edged away from Pierce.

"Thanks man," Pierce told Malachi as he and Ethan moved away from the counter. A few of the kids had formed a line at the snack counter but most everyone was still huddled around the mall benches outside of the theater. Ethan wasted no time in tearing open several candy bars and chowing down. Pierce noticed that Ethan had forgotten his soda back at the snack counter. Just watching Ethan down all that candy made Pierce feel sick, so he decided not to remind him about the soda he left on the counter.

There was no room on the benches outside so Ethan and Pierce had sat on a bench inside the theater where they could eat their candy in peace. They had been sitting there for about two minutes when Micah walked over to them. Micah was tall and lanky, which always intimidated Pierce.

"Hey guys," Micah began, "David should be back from Sears any minute now, and I doubt they will be bringing good news. I think we need to prepare for the fact that we might be spending the night in the mall." Micah stopped to let Ethan and Pierce digest what he had said. Ethan froze with a Snickers sticking halfway out of his mouth. Pierce was less surprised.

Micah continued, "If the line at the snack counter tells me anything, I bet everyone is hungry. I was thinking that maybe you, Ethan, Bailey and Hannah could scout out the food court and see what is available for dinner tonight. The rest of us will wait for David here at the theater, then meet you in the food court to eat and plan our next move," Micah stared directly at Pierce. "Can you do that?"

Pierce thought Micah was being a little rude to Ethan, but he had been thinking along the same lines for awhile now. A slice of pizza sounded more satisfying than the tub of candy bars Ethan was still clutching protectively.

"Sure," Pierce replied. "Did you already talk to Bailey and Hannah?"

"Yep. They are ready and waiting for you guys. Bailey has a flashlight for each of you just in case the power goes out and I gave Hannah one of our Walkie Talkies." replied Micah. Micah's response was so quick Pierce could tell he had obviously been planning this for awhile. Pierce wondered what else Micah had up his sleeve. With that, Micah made an efficient turn and headed back to the main group of kids without so much as a word of thanks.

"Well, Ethan, shall we?" Pierce jumped up without waiting for Ethan's agreement and started walking toward Bailey and Hannah. Ethan look confounded for a moment, but then followed willingly as he continued to munch on the king-size Snickers bar.

Bailey and Hannah made quite the contrast standing next to one another. Bailey was tall and chubby, while in contrast Hannah was petite and athletic. Pierce knew that they were not best friends, but had grown up in the same neighborhood and had a comfortable friendship. He offered them a smile as he approached them. Pierce noticed that Hannah was staring curiously at the tub of candy Ethan was carrying.

"So we are the chosen ones, aye?" Pierce asked.

Hannah and Bailey both responded with a smile. His comment helped break the ice.

"I think Micah is right, most of us have not eaten any real food since lunch today." Hannah offered, looking pointedly at Ethan's candy.

Ethan finally caught on to her criticism and offered up a response as they started walking. "At least Snickers have peanuts for protein!" he responded in his defense.

Pierce had to smile and so did the girls.

They made their way down the hall and approached the food court. Pierce had been feeling so good about getting up to do something about their predicament that he was not ready for the strange scene before them. Normally the food court was full of hungry shoppers munching on fast food and sipping large soda pops. Instead the half eaten food was laying on tables. The chairs were neither tipped over nor neatly pushed in. It was impossible to tell if people either left their food in a calm evacuation or simply disappeared into thin air. A few jackets and coats lay scattered about the room.

"Whoa," Bailey said quietly, "I wasn't expecting this. What happened to all of the people?"

"It is weird," Hannah replied. "It's like everyone just agreed to get up and leave all at once."

Pierce was just as weirded out as the girls. The only way to ease his anxiety was to jump into work mode. He took a minute to look around. First he surveyed the restaurants. On the right hand corner was the large pizza chain Sbarro's. Behind a long Plexiglas window was a counter covered by bright lights keeping five pizzas warm. Next to the pizza were dishes full of lasagna, pasta, and breadsticks. Although the pizza might be three or four hours old it should still be edible - at least as edible as gas station food. His stomach rumbled. Four hour old pizza sounded just fine to him.

Pierce then looked around at their other choices. There was a Panda Express, an Ichiban, a Taco Time, McDonalds, Burger King, Subway, and three local specialty shops. Pierce knew that almost every store would have a warming section with pre-prepared food just ready to eat. Like the pizza, it might be a little stale, but still edible, and he knew exactly what they should do next.

"I think Micah wanted us to get the food ready for everyone so we could eat quickly and talk about what to do next. If we are going to spend the night in the mall we might as well do so on a full stomach. Besides, finding a way out of here might take some real brainpower," Pierce mused. He looked around and saw that Bailey and Hannah were listening politely. Ethan had set his popcorn tub down, but was still unconsciously popping M&M's into his mouth.

Pierce continued, "So…I think I have a plan, let me know what you think. Sbarro's has a large section of counter under the warming lights. I think we should split up and see what hot edible food we can get from each place. We can bring the food back here and arrange it next to the pizzas. That way when everyone comes to eat they can just see what is available and get what they want without having to search all the restaurants. We don't want total chaos when they arrive." Pierce smiled mischievously at the thought of a food free for all.

"Good idea," Bailey nodded thoughtfully, and then added, "I would like to clean up the food off of these tables and create a space where we can eat and think together, it creeped me out to see the abandoned food when I first walked in here.

"Great idea!" Hannah chimed in. "I think the three of us can gather the food if you want to clean up a few tables Bailey. Do you guys mind if I start at the restaurants over there and work my way over?" Hannah pointed directly across the room to Subway.

"Sounds good," Pierce agreed. "Where do you want to start, Ethan?"

Ethan looked around before responding. "Let me take McDonalds, Taco Time, and the other sandwich place."

"Let's do this," said Peirce.

Pierce was glad that the food court was a large open room. They could scout out the whole area while still staying within sight of one another. Hannah and Ethan headed out to their prospective restaurants while Bailey picked up a tray and started clearing away the uneaten food. Pierce figured he would begin at the spot right next to Sbarro's, then work his way down the row and meet Hannah in the middle.

He approached the Burger King storefront when he realized that there was no entry into the place. None of the food joints had doors, as the employees entered and exited through the back and served behind the counter. He glanced back self consciously to see Hannah effortlessly vault herself over the counter at Subway.

Well, there was no other way to do it. Somewhat less gracefully, he pulled himself up on the counter like he was getting out of a swimming pool, and dropped down the other side. He was now inside the mall version of Burger King. Pierce got right to work, and grabbed a tray from next to the cashier stand. Out of the corner of his eye he caught sight of a box of plastic gloves. He bet Bailey would appreciate those so he poked his head out over the counter and yelled out.

"Hey Bailey! I found some plastic gloves you could use!"

Bailey looked up, smiled, then held up her hands ruefully. "I didn't even think of how dirty they must be. Eww! Let me go wash my hands in the bathroom and I will be right back." Bailey started toward the mall bathrooms then slowed down. She turned around and came back to the Burger King counter where Pierce had set the box of gloves.

"Hey Pierce, do they have a sink for hand washing in the back of Burger King?" Bailey asked. Pierce had started to stack wrapped burgers from the warming rail on his tray. He jumped at the sound of Bailey's voice.

"Um, yeah, I'm sure they do. Let me go look." Pierce set his tray on the counter and started toward the back as Bailey climbed over the counter. Sure enough, there was a hand washing station across from the dishwashing sink.

"I might as well wash my hands while I am here…should have thought of that before." Pierce added with a sheepish grin. He should know better than to touch food without first washing his hands.

He let Bailey wash her hands first as he looked around the kitchen area. There were large grills, stations for making different food items, and a long wall of deep fryers. He had passed the fry area on the way back. A huge pile of fries lay under warming light waiting to be packaged into small and large portions.

Bailey finished washing her hands and moved out of Pierce's way while she dried them on a paper towel.

"Back to work," she said with a smile and headed toward the front. Pierce watched as she passed the fries. She reached out and grabbed a few with her freshly cleaned hands.

"I might as well try a few of these," Bailey remarked as she bit into a few hot ones. She grimaced as she chewed.

"Well…." Pierce asked expectantly.

"Edible, but definitely stale. Kind of like our school lunch fries!" She looked around. "I'll remember to get some ketchup and other condiments." Bailey then cleared the counter with a quick jump (her height being an advantage) grabbed a few pairs of gloves and headed back to her cleaning.

Pierce followed Bailey's lead and used a pair of plastic gloves to gather the hot food. So far he had three Whoppers, four chicken sandwiches, and five miscellaneous hot sandwiches. He went over to the fry station and tasted a few of the fries himself. (Bailey was correct....they were edible just not super fresh and lacking salt.) He looked around and found a large salt shaker above the station. Carefully he added a few-well placed shakes to the pile of fries while mixing them with his other hand.

Pierce always wondered what it would be like to work in a fast food restaurant. His parent's restaurant had some equipment that was similar to what he saw here at Burger King, but many of the appliances were just different enough that he would have to do some research before he could operate them properly. He looked curiously over at the deep fryer. The basic mechanisms were obvious, but he was not sure where the timer and temperature screens were located. It appeared that this deep fryer was made exclusively for making Burger King fries. He used the metal scooper to fill up large size fry containers and stacked them neatly on the tray next to the pile of burgers. Pierce looked around briefly but did not see anything else worth grabbing.

He was the first to return to the Sbarro's with a tray of food. He saw that Bailey had already cleaned off twenty or so tables. She looked up at Pierce as he was jumping over the counter of the Sbarro's with his tray.

He saw Bailey reach up and wipe the sweat off of her face. Pierce realized she must have been working hard - really hard.

"Pierce, would you look for some towels or rags in the Sbarro's that I could use to wipe down these tables?" Bailey then pointed toward the spilled soda and splotches of ketchup. Mall patrons were not known for their fastidious habits.

"No problem," Pierce replied. He set his tray of burgers and fries next to a pizza on a warming tray and went to look for something Bailey could use to wipe down the tables. He walked to the back, quickly found several white towels, wet them under the sink, and handed them to Bailey across the counter.

Next Pierce surveyed the warming lights at the pizza counter. The pizzas were already cut and ready to serve. He could just slide the five pizzas closer together on one side of the counter and make room for other food. Pierce moved the pizzas and then arranged his burgers by type next to the last pizza.

He also noticed that Sbarro's did not have fountain soft drinks but instead sold bottled soda, juice, and water. There was a small supply of bottled drinks sitting in a bin of ice next to the cashier's area. Pierce counted eighteen drinks. He went to the back of the store and looked in the supply closet. Score! There were cases of bottled water, soda, and juice stacked up high to the ceiling. If they were stuck in the mall for any prolonged period of time they would have plenty to drink, and every restaurant in the food court was probably similarly supplied. He grabbed one case of each drink and carried them up to the front. Pierce knew they would all need water so he stocked the ice bin to the brim. They would probably still be lukewarm when everyone arrived, but it was better than nothing.

Before he left to raid the next eatery, Pierce went back into the pizza kitchen. He watched the track as it rolled around in the hot oven. Both his cooking instincts and his yearning not to waste electricity caused him to reach up and turn off the oven. It slowly rolled to a stop and suddenly the kitchen was quiet.

Satisfied, he pulled himself up and over the counter once again. Pierce was beginning to get the hang of crossing the counters without appearing to be a total oaf.

It took another twenty minutes to finish gathering all the food. As he worked he daydreamed about what it would be like if he had all these kitchens and all the ingredients to make whatever he wanted. The possibilities would be endless

CHAPTER 8
DINNERTIME

Bailey had to admit she was having fun. The empty food court had weirded her out and the possibility of being alone freaked her out, so when Pierce suggested they split up and scavenge food from the different fast food joints Bailey asked to clear the tables. Staying behind to tidy up was the perfect excuse to avoid being alone. By washing the tables she could keep everyone in sight as they retrieved food from the surrounding restaurants.

She was thankful Pierce found her plastic gloves, it made picking up half eaten food that much easier. Unlike the untouched food sitting under warming lights, the abandoned food on the food court tables was disgusting. Everything was half eaten and messy.

Bailey was sickened with the amount of food some people ordered. She couldn't tell for sure but she thought one mall patron must have ordered two slices of pizza AND two cheeseburgers, a large fry and a soda. Bailey was by no means a light or healthy eater…but she wasn't a pig either.

After she donned the gloves she timed herself and cleaned seven tables in one minute. Looking around the room, she found one of the custodians garbage cans on wheels sitting conveniently nearby. It was easier for her to wheel the can around and dump trays, instead of carrying the trays to a stationary garbage can. By the time she had cleaned over forty or so odd tables, the garbage can was piled high with trash.

Just as she realized how dirty the empty tables were, she saw Pierce jumping over the counter of Sbarro's with a tray of Burger King food. Bailey called out and asked Pierce to get her some rags to wipe off the tables. He was quick to oblige.

As she cleaned off each table she realized that she could do more to make the area more inviting. The large open food court was cold and unwelcoming. Even though the place was brightly lit, it was missing the light from the large skylights. The dark night sky gave the room an ominous feeling.

Bailey paused and looked up. The reality was it was impossible to tell if the skylights were looking out on a dark night sky or covered up with twenty feet of snow. If there was twenty feet of snow outside of the mall wouldn't there logically be twenty feet of snow on top of the roof?

Bailey shivered…if there was that much snow on top wouldn't the weight of the snow cause the skylights and roof to collapse? Then she shrugged, she could not hear any sound indicating an imminent collapse so she might as well ignore the possibility.

It was weird enough that she was clearing food from tables in an empty food court, but she could counteract some of this weirdness and her own nervousness by creating a sense of 'home' in the food court.

To start Bailey decided to move the tables into a long row. She counted out the appropriate amount of tables and chairs she would need to make a table long enough to seat all of her classmates. There were twenty-eight students in her class so she could create a long rectangular table easy enough.

After moving the first table she realized that they were extremely heavy tables - it was more difficult than she expected. She decided to keep moving the tables even if it was just a few inches at a time. When she was done she had worked up quite a sweat. Stepping back she admired her work. The table she created was long and wide, reminding her of those large dining tables that you would find in the hall of a castle or mansion.

Next Bailey remembered seeing the French fries from Burger King and thinking they would need ketchup. Since everyone else was gathering up hot food she doubted they would be thinking about utensils, condiments, or napkins. Looking across the room Pierce was heading over to Cinnabon and she could see Hannah moving across the way to Yama Sushi next to Subway. Bailey craned her neck and looked in the direction she thought Ethan should be, but couldn't see him anywhere from her vantage point.

First she would tackle utensils. Not wanting to stray far from the Sbarro's, Bailey hopped over the counter and checked out what they had to offer. Unlike some places that had condiment stations out front for the public to use, Sbarro's kept all their accessories behind the counter. She found a stack of plates, napkins, forks, knives and spoons. Sbarro's used sturdy plastic silverware instead of the cheap stuff she had expected.

As she was gathering up supplies she noticed that Pierce crammed as many bottled waters into the ice bin as he possibly could. She blew through her lips in exasperation. Pierce had good intentions, but he did a really sloppy job. Almost all the water bottles he had added were above the ice line, they wouldn't get cold that way.

Since the other kids were likely to show up in ten or twenty minutes, Bailey removed all the water bottles and dug out the ones that had been sitting in the ice for hours. These she put to the side and replaced them with the new warm water bottles and juices. Grabbing as many cold drinks as she could carry, she placed the water bottles around the table at even intervals. This gave her an idea. She could set the table and make it look inviting!

Inspired, she grabbed the napkins, forks, knives, and spoons. There was no time to fold the napkins in a fancy manner, but at least she could give each seat a proper table setting. Most people would probably not need plastic utensils to eat but none of this dissuaded her from setting the table. In no time she had the table ready to go.

Baliey paused again before tackling the condiments. She was letting her eyes drift around the building from storefront to storefront where she caught a glimpse of flowers. Flowers? They must be plastic. She ran over and reached across the counter. Perfect! Potted fake flowers would be the icing on her table top. As she reached for the second vase a face popped up from behind the counter. It took her a second to register who it was.

"Pierce!" she screamed. He had obviously seen her coming and ducked behind the counter before she arrived.

"Sorry," he said somewhat apologetically, although Bailey could still see his eyes dancing merrily behind his sober expression.

"It's ok," she said gasping between breaths, "You just scared the heck out of me!"

"Boo!" came a half-hearted attempt at scaring her from behind her left shoulder. This time she recognized Hannah's voice immediately, although she hadn't heard any footsteps.

"Hannah, I know it's you," Bailey admonished as she turned to look at her old friend. Bailey and Hannah had known one another since they were two years old. They grew up in the same neighborhood but rarely hung out these days as their lives were so different. Yet nothing could erase the years of playing together when they were younger. Because they rarely talked, most people did not know how close they had once been or that they were even friends.

"I know, I know, but I heard the scream from next door and couldn't resist joining in on the fun," Hannah replied with a smile and a wink.

"So what have you found, Hannah?" asked Pierce.

"Well, Subway didn't have anything pre-prepared, so I started to make one turkey sandwich but the whole process was way too time consuming. However, I did grab some chips and all the cookies from the front." To illustrate her point she held up a large see through plastic bag stuffed with chips and cookies. "Then I checked out the sushi place next door. I have a whole tray with about twenty sushi rolls sitting in the cooler ready to go when we need them. Since sushi needs to stay cool I figured we could bring it over when we are ready to eat. I'm guessing not that many people like sushi, but I love it!"

"Eww! I never understood how people could eat raw fish," Bailey said with a grimace. Hannah smiled back once again.

The two of us are really soooo different, Bailey thought as she looked at Hannah.

"Next I went to KFC and scored three huge buckets of chicken, a bunch of popcorn chicken, some mashed potatoes, and another tub of biscuits." Hannah pointed to where she had set the tray of hot food on a table behind her. The chicken buckets were stacked three high. Bailey wondered how Hannah managed to walk the stack all the way over without them tipping over. The KFC aroma wafted under her nose as her stomach rumbled.

"I see you didn't do too shabby yourself, Pierce." Hannah said. She pointed to a large tower of to-go boxes sitting on the counter next to Pierce.

"I know! I scored at Panda Express by cleaning out the warming trays that were filled with all sorts of good stuff. We have chow mien, orange chicken, pot stickers, and at least ten other dishes." Pierce looked at his tower of food and then looked over at Bailey. "Would you mind helping me carry this?" he asked.

Bailey quickly set down the fake flowers she had been intending to take and reached for the top five to-go boxes.

"Oh, you were going to bring those flowers weren't you?" Pierce asked.

"Yeah, but I can come back for them after we get this food under the heat lights." replied Bailey.

The three of them made their way slowly across the food court. Hannah was swaying under her burden of stacked chicken buckets. As they approached Sbarro's, Pierce spotted the large table Bailey set and gave a low appreciative whistle.

"Pretty fancy, now I understand why you were getting the flowers." Pierce said. Bailey gave him an inquisitive look. She did not know Pierce that well, so she was unsure if this was a compliment or not. It was hard to tell by the intonation of his voice.

After setting the to-go containers down on the counter, Bailey returned to get the flowers while Hannah and Pierce climbed over the counter and arranged the hot food. When Bailey returned they were still organizing all the fast food into neat little rows.

It was strange to see so many different types of fast food all in one place. There was a stack of burgers next to a line of fries followed by large buckets of chicken sitting next to several kinds of Chinese dishes. This would be any kids dream. Getting to pick pizza, burgers, and KFC all at the same meal! Her classmates were going to be thrilled when they came into the food court. Hopefully they could ignore the slight staleness of the food.

While she was getting the flowers she jumped over the counter at the Panda Express and grabbed a large handful of chopsticks. Right next to the chopsticks she saw a huge cardboard box of fortune cookies. Cool! She threw the chopsticks on top of the box and lugged the whole thing up to the counter. She might as well bring the whole box over to the dinner table. Bailey also managed to put the flower vases on top of the fortune cookies so she would only have to make one trip.

After arranging the flowers she dragged a few more tables together to create a place for the chopsticks, fortune cookies, and other condiments.

"What other stuff do you think we will need other than soy sauce?" Bailey asked Pierce and Hannah. All three of them glanced down at the rows of hot food.

"Ketchup, mustard, mayonnaise, salt, and pepper," Pierce said but his list was cut short by a loud noise coming from Hannah's pocket.

"I almost forgot!" Hannah's hands flew to her face momentarily, "the Walkie Talkie!" Hannah grabbed frantically at her belt to remove the Walkie Talkie and held it up high for all to listen.

"Hannah, are you there?" a voice that sounded like Micah's crackled out of the Walkie Talkie. Hannah fumbled with the controls as she tried to figure out how to respond. Pierce gently reached over and helped her press down the talk button.

"Hannah here. Micah is that you?" Hannah replied into the Walkie Talkie, her voice unnaturally loud.

"Yes this is Micah. David and the others have still not arrived. If they don't show up in the next five minutes we are going to head down your way and figure out what to do next. Did you guys find enough food?" Micah's voice crackled, but was still audible.

"Um, we didn't find anything out of the ordinary, and yes," Hannah paused as she looked at the pile of pizzas, burgers, and assorted fast food, "we found PLENTY of food for everyone," As Hannah finished speaking into the Walkie Talkie Bailey noticed that Ethan was heading their way carrying a tray piled high with more food. Bailey started walking toward Ethan so she could help him, but made sure to stay close enough to hear what Micah was saying.

"Sounds good. Over and out." Micah replied.

"Um, over and out." Hannah said in her raised voice.

"Wow Ethan! You brought back quite the haul!" Bailey complemented Ethan as he approached. She could tell that he had been feeling a little down earlier and all those candy bars he had eaten couldn't have helped. Ethan set down his tray on Sbarro's counter as he surveyed what Pierce and Hannah had gathered. Bailey hoped he was not feeling like he needed to compete with them.

"I have two more fully loaded trays back at Taco Time. Anyone want to come help me carry them?" asked Ethan.

"I will," Bailey swiftly replied, "let's go before the food gets cold." Ethan looked relieved at her offer and they both set out toward Taco Time. As they got closer Bailey realized that Ethan wasn't kidding when he said he had two more full trays of food. Ethan even loaded up on desserts and snacks from both places.

They each picked up a heavy tray and carefully made their way back to Sbarro's. When they arrived Bailey set her tray down momentarily on the table. Hannah and Pierce were nowhere to be seen. Ethan didn't notice, as his attention was focused on the table Bailey set.

"Nice job, Bailey! You went out of your way to set the table!" Bailey enjoyed his compliment although she did feel a little crazy. Here they were, in the middle of some type of major emergency, and she was spending time setting a fancy table? Maybe she had gone a little too far. She hoped her other classmates would feel the same as Ethan and appreciate her hard work.

Just then Ethan noticed that Hannah and Pierce were missing. "Where did they disappear…." his sentence was interrupted as the pair emerged from A&W carrying what appeared to be a tray of root beer floats.

Pierce smiled over at Ethan. "We figured everyone would be ready for dessert as well. Besides, I didn't want anyone to threaten your popcorn tub full of candy."

Ethan looked a little peeved but after being surrounded by all this excess fast food his tub full of candy paled in comparison. Ethan shook it off and held up a handful of apple pies.

"I was thinking just the same thing!" he said matching their grins.

Hannah took charge. "Everyone else will be here any second now. I sure hope David and the rest have shown up, although we probably would have seen them walk down the hall over there as they passed by to return to the theater. Did any of you see them by any chance?" She asked.

"Don't worry," Bailey assured her. "It would have been easy for them to pass by unnoticed. We haven't been very loud because we were focusing on our work." With those words the four of them looked around. They had accomplished much in the last half hour. They started to hop back into Sbarro's to organize the last two trays of food when Bailey heard noises from the far side of the food court. Glancing up in apprehension, she was relieved to see her classmates arriving.

"You guys finish up putting the food away. I am going to go see if David made it back from Sears," Hannah said in a bossy tone of voice. Now Bailey remembered why she and Hannah were so different. Hannah was an amazing athlete, but her strength on the playing field translated into everyday bossiness. Bailey grimaced to herself, but did not complain out loud. They would all hear the news soon enough.

Behind the counter Pierce took charge. Bailey did not mind following his lead, he was an entirely different leader compared to Hannah. She watched Pierce carefully as he looked around Sbarro's.

"Would you guys mind helping me serve as everyone comes through the line for food?" Pierce looked at Bailey and Ethan as he waited for a response.

"No problem," they replied in unison, then looked at each other, and laughed.

"Great," Pierce said, "We can put the cold items on top of this section of the counter, so people can grab what they need. The only items we will need to actually serve will be the main dishes sitting under the hot lights," here he paused, "Oh yeah, I forgot. Hannah left some sushi back over at the sushi place. You guys keep setting up while I grab the sushi." Bailey watched as Pierce vaulted the counter and headed across the food court. She then turned back toward Ethan and helped him organize the last few items.

She and Ethan were so busy they hardly noticed classmates walking slowly across the food court. The new arrivals were unusually quiet as they took in the scene around them. Wrappers, half-eaten entrées, and tall sodas littered almost every table in the room except the ones Bailey cleared off.

When the students arrived at Sbarro's Bailey was done organizing the food and took some time to look around. She was relieved to see everyone who went to Sears made it back safely. It was then that she realized, she hadn't expected them to have any success in the first place. Bailey's intuition told her that they were going to be stuck in the mall for a long time.

Hannah was talking to Micah and David who were the focal points of the group. They were looking at the table and then in Bailey's direction and they looked pleased. She wondered if Hannah told them she was the one with the idea to set a table.

It did not take very long for the students to forget about the weird empty room and hone in on the plethora of fast food in front of them. Bailey checked her phone for the time and saw that it was indeed seven-fifteen. The class was supposed to be on the bus and halfway to their home in Canada right now. Instead, they were about to eat a stale fast food feast in an empty mall. Life was weird. She felt like she was living out some preposterous movie.

David, Micah and Hannah walked around the edge of the crowd and met up with David who was returning with a tray full of sushi. Bailey was glad she grabbed chopsticks earlier.

The crowd moved closer to the Sbarro's counter and were looking over all the food options. Lindsey was standing right across the counter from Bailey. She watched as Lindsey's eyes lit up while scanning the fast food. It was like going to a school that served unlimited fast food. (Never mind the staleness – school food was bad enough that the comparison was still a good one.) Bailey grinned at Lindsey.

"You don't have to decide what you want Lindsey, there is enough here that you can have a little bit of everything," Bailey spoke over the tall glass counter. Lindsey smiled back and continued to eye the food without saying anything.

David spoke up, "Hey guys. Hannah, Pierce, Ethan and Bailey gathered all the hot food into one place and set this table for us. We were thinking that we would eat and then make a plan for what to do next. Pierce, give us directions on how to dish up."

Pierce looked excited, and he started to gesture while giving instructions. "We collected all the hot food under the pizza lights. It is already a little stale, but still edible. Feel free to eat as much as you like, I doubt it would taste very good tomorrow even if refrigerated.

We also gathered some cold food such as sushi and root beer floats. I made the root beer floats awhile ago so grab them early as they may be getting mushy." Here Pierce paused and pointed to the cashier area, "Here are some trays. Form a line over here. Bailey, Ethan, and I will serve the hot food for you. Feel free to grab any of the cold items yourself. Drinks are on the table and in the ice bin."

It didn't take long for the students to get in line and start asking for food. David took the stack of trays to the end of the counter and then went back to join Ethan and Bailey. Bailey was already standing by the Chinese food so she decided to serve those dishes, as well as the pizzas to her right. Looking around, she saw a serving spoon stuck in a pasta dish. She decided to use that to serve the Chinese food. Ethan was already at her left near the food he had procured, so Pierce took charge of serving the food on her far right.

The first students were hesitant, but as everyone began to get comfortable with the idea, their voices rose and it made the situation less tense. It almost sounded like a normal day in the school cafeteria, except that the room was ten times as big and the ceiling four times as tall. Their voices echoed quietly against the food court ceiling.

Bailey quickly became efficient at dishing up the Chinese food. Pierce anticipated that they would need plates for the pizza and Chinese food, so he gave Bailey a stack of paper plates. As the kids came through the line she saw trays piled high with cheese burgers, fries, tater tots, tacos, and desserts.

Malachi already had so much stuff on his tray that he decided to set his tray at the table and get back in line for a second round of food. Luke decided to try a little bit of everything. He asked Bailey to give him one spoonful of each Chinese dish. She had scooped a little bit of each entrée until his plate was full to the brim.

Only a handful of students limited themselves to a modest amount of food. Brittany asked for extra small portions, and Micah also appeared to be a light eater. Micah had been one of the first in line, but he was nibbling at his food as he talked intently with David - he must have a plan in mind.

The line began to wind down with about half of the kids going through twice. Tanner, who was tall and buff, actually finished all the food on his first tray and was coming through a second time for more pizza. Bailey was getting hungry watching everyone else eat.

Pierce spoke up just as Bailey's belly growled loudly, "Hey guys, why don't you dish up yourselves and eat. I'll stay here and serve people." He then grabbed some French fries and started munching. Bailey was thankful for Pierce's suggestion. She grabbed a tray and filled it up with burgers and pizza. For some reason, she was craving comfort food tonight. Grabbing a soda she jumped over the counter and went to sit in one of the few free seats at the table. As she was sitting down, David stood up to speak so he could be heard all along the table.

"I don't even know how to start. This is one of the strangest experiences I have ever had. I would say I was dreaming, but no matter what I try to do I can't wake up." David stopped here and looked around at his fellow classmates. They fell silent, with a few students still chewing on their food. Many who had initially thought they were hungry discovered their stomachs were now queasy.

Bailey looked around with a quiet contentedness as David began to speak again. This may be a crazy situation, but she had done her part to make life better. All of a sudden, she was not just the poor girl in class who Brittany made fun of at every opportunity. Bailey was the one who thought of arranging the tables into one big table. Here, in an empty mall, she had a chance to be someone else, to find a different spot on the pecking order. Bailey didn't know what to expect next, but as she looked at the faces of her classmates around her, she couldn't help think life might be a little different if they were stuck in a mall for awhile.

CHAPTER 9
FOUND

Zoe had been sticking close to Miel since they worked together in Sears. So when it came time to sit down to eat, Zoe was quick to take a seat next to her. Even though she didn't feel like eating much, she was thrilled to get to pick and choose from the food available. KFC, Taco Time, and McDonalds all in one sitting! Back at home her parents rarely took them out to fast food, and when they did get to eat out, they were only allowed to order from the cheap menus. Now she could have everything she wanted!

As one of the last kids in line, Zoe didn't mind taking a huge portion of fried chicken, three Big Macs, and several beef and bean burritos, even though she knew there was no way she could eat them all!

She noticed that Miel didn't grab a root beer float, so she brought an extra one to the table in case it was an oversight.

"I brought you a root beer float, Miel," Zoe offered as she plopped down in the next seat.

"Thanks," Miel replied dismissively with a faraway look on her face. At first Zoe took offense, but then she realized Miel was just thinking really hard. Zoe used this time to study her friend. Miel was still wearing the mittens and gloves they had picked up at Sears. She also had her handbag from school wrapped protectively around one leg. It must be out of habit, as no one here was going to try and steal her bag, especially at a time like this. Miel's tray held two pieces of cheese pizza and a large French fry. It was then that Zoe remembered Miel was a vegetarian.

It didn't seem like a good time to bother Miel, so Zoe got down to business and started eating her food. She managed to finish a chicken wing, one burrito, and half of a Big Mac before she couldn't eat anymore. For a second she felt bad about taking such a big portion, but when she looked back at where Pierce was hovering over the food, it was easy to see that there were still plenty of leftovers. She pushed her tray away and started stirring the root beer float with her spoon. Pierce was right, almost all of the ice cream had melted into the root beer. She wondered if this is where soda companies got the idea for cream soda. Even though the ice cream melted it was still yummy.

As she finished eating David began to speak. Zoe thought he was kinda cute, in a nerdy sort of way. She was not surprised in the slightest that he was taking a leadership role. David was well liked by almost everyone and Miss. Schmidt always put him in charge of things, so this was a natural extension of his personality. She quietly sipped on her cream soda and listened carefully.

"I think most of you have heard what happened at Sears. The snow was piled slightly less high on the upper level parking lot. There seemed to be a steady wind outside that may have kept the roof and upper levels of the parking garage from being completely buried. We still can't tell how much snow is on the roof." With this comment David looked and pointed up at the skylights above them. "If they were buried in snow I bet they would have caved in by now, but they haven't, so we're very lucky."

"Why are our phones not working?" Brittany asked, with an undertone that was both annoyed and scared.

"That is one of many questions we don't have any answers for. At this point in time I don't think asking those kinds of questions is going to help our situation. We need to take quick action. If we end up being stuck here for any extended period of time we will have lots of time to think about things like that. But right now, we need to act."

"I have been talking with Micah and several of you about what we need to do. Some ideas we have include trying to find a land line that would allow us to call or connect with the internet. It is obvious our wireless connections are not working." With that comment, several students pulled out their cell phones and checked for service for the millionth time. Zoe almost laughed out loud. Like their cell phone service was suddenly just going to reappear. Zoe let her cell phone stay right where it was – in her pocket.

"In addition to trying to find a way to communicate with the outside world, I think we need to search the mall for other survivors. If we were left behind, it is highly likely there are a few other people still here too. This is a big mall and they may simply be on the other side of the mall." Here David paused and looked around to see how the students were reacting. Most faces were impassive as they took in what he said.

"This is the plan we have come up with after counting people and supplies. We split up into groups of four people and every group gets a Walkie Talkie and two flashlights. Each group will be assigned a section of the mall to search. One of the groups will have special assignment. Their job will be to check the Apple Store for land lines." He paused again then continued, "This search may take half the night, but I think it will be well worth it if we can find other people. If not, at least we will know we are all alone. So… what do you guys think of that plan?" Pierce opened the floor for discussion.

No one spoke for a few minutes. Many were sucking on the dregs of their root beer floats.

Tyler broke the silence. "I would like to go with the communications group."

At that Brittany jumped in, "I want to search the clothing stores!"

"We will be searching by section, not type of store. It would be too complicated to split our searches up in that way." Micah retorted, even though he was usually not the type to speak suddenly, much less challenge Brittany of all people.

"Hey! I think I have something that can help!" Pierce stuck his head out of the back room of Sbarro's. "Give me a second…."

"Shall we do a show of hands to get an idea of what we think?" David asked. Zoe though this was a wise decision. Nobody seemed willing to speak up and defy Brittany or support David.

"Who would like to help out with the search parties?" David asked. It did not take long for everyone to raise their hands. There was not a single dissenter, even though Brittany looked a little put out by Micah's admonishment. "Well, looks like we have a plan for the early evening at least. I wonder where we should have our home base?" David inquired.

"We could have the home base right here?" suggested Victoria. "Then we wouldn't have to go far for food."

Zoe had another idea. "We may actually get tired later tonight. What about setting up home base someplace where there are a lot of beds? That way if some people finish early they can get some sleep while they are waiting for other groups to return?"

"Like any of us are going to get sleep tonight," Tanner interjected.

"I know, but it still might be nice to have a place to lay down. And even though all the food is here, the food court is kind of creepy with all the leftovers sitting around." Zoe pointed out. This seemed to be a good suggestion, as Zoe and her classmates looked around the cluttered food court. A large room with a bunch of half eaten food just wasn't very inviting. And besides, thought Zoe, at some point the food was going to start stinking up the place. It might not happen for a few days, but getting rescued in the next few hours seemed less and less likely.

"I agree," said Hannah, "maybe we could use Sleep City. I think it is up on the second floor."

“Good idea” David approved. “Any other suggestions?”

“Well, what about Sears?” Miel asked, “I was thinking that we should continue trying to dig out once the sun rises tomorrow, if we don’t have any other luck escaping. And at Sears they have mattresses, blankets, pillows, tools, and almost anything we might need except food. The food court is more centrally located, but if we go to Sleep City we will have to go much further for our bedding. At least at Sears we have lots of supplies without having to be spread out all over the place.” Whew. Zoe heard Miel draw in a sharp breath. She had given the whole speech without a pause.

Zoe liked Miel’s idea. As usual Miel was thinking ahead, she was so practical and smart. Zoe decided then and there that she was going to stick close to Miel.

David looked at Micah out of the corner of his eye. He then looked at Cody, Tanner, Luke and then continued his gaze around the rest of the table before speaking. “Good thinking Miel, let’s make Sears our home base for the time being. Pierce can be in charge of bringing some snacks back to Sears after his group is done searching.” David looked up at this point as Pierce had returned from the back of Sbarro’s and was standing behind Cody. In his arms David held some dry erase markers, an eraser, a notepad, and several pens.

“I was thinking that we could use the dry erase pens to mark the sections we are going to search on that mall map over there,” Pierce waved his hand in the direction of the large plastic mall map in the food court entrance. “And we can use the pens and paper for any other sort of recordkeeping. I figure, if we are going to do an effective search we might as well be well organized.” Pierce smiled, organization outside of the kitchen was not his normal strength. But something about this situation was bringing out the best in him. “And I’ll gather snacks to bring back to Sears.” He nodded at David to let him know he was done speaking.

“Well, any other thoughts before we get started?” David asked the group.

Usually her classmates were more argumentative than this. The strange events and long day must have made them particularly docile, Zoe thought.

"Micah, do you mind being in charge of organizing and recording the search parties on the mall map?" David asked. "And Hannah, would you record everything Micah writes on the mall map on paper so that when we return to Sears we'll have a copy of where each group searched?"

David then turned and addressed Victoria. "Lastly, Victoria will be in charge of distributing the flashlights and Walkie Talkies once the groups are formed. Everyone choose their own groups and check in with Micah once you have four people."

To Zoe, it felt just like a day at school when the teacher asked you to form your own groups. Some people predictably paired together, while other people looked around waiting for someone to ask them. Zoe knew she wanted to be in Miel's group, so she jumped on the chance.

"Miel, do you want to be in a group with me?" Zoe asked.

"Sure, um, who else?" responded Miel, still with that faraway look in her eyes.

Zoe looked around the room to see who should be in their group. She could see that Molly, Brittany, and Lindsey were joined at the hip looking for a third person. Cody, Tanner, Luke, and David were also a predictable grouping. Tyler was talking to Micah about something. Malachi had wandered in the direction of Nolan and Ethan. She spotted Emily and Madison still sitting in the middle of the table finishing a pound of French fries. How Emily managed to keep her skin so clear after eating all that grease Zoe had no idea. Eating fast food nearly guaranteed Zoe that her face would break out for the next two weeks.

"Madison!" Zoe called out loudly. She wanted to get to that pair before anyone else did. She jumped up and made her way over to where the two girls were sitting. "Miel and I were wondering if you would like to make a group of four?"

"Sure," Madison replied. Emily didn't look too pleased that Madison agreed to partner up, but she didn't say anything. Zoe could never quite figure Emily out. She was drop dead gorgeous and all the guys liked her, but she didn't get along with anyone at school. She had no best friends, and had never shown any interest in the guys who adored her.

"I'll get Miel and we will come join you guys while you finish your fries." Zoe informed them. She turned around and went back to find Miel tidying up both her and Zoe's tray. Zoe thanked Miel and they tossed their garbage in a nearby receptacle. "Madison and Emily will search with us. Is that alright?"

"Oh, sure," replied Miel, "Let's get some water bottles or juice to take with us." Zoe followed Miel over to Sbarro's counter and grabbed some drinks for the four of them out of the ice bin. They then walked over to Madison and Emily in silence. Zoe wished Miel would snap out of her deep thinking mode. Ah well. Zoe would have to hold up Miel's end of the conversation until she was ready to speak up.

"You guys ready?" Zoe asked. The girls had finished off every last fry, so the question was kind of redundant.

"Yup!" replied Madison enthusiastically, "I am actually kind of excited to get moving and check the mall out. It does seem likely that there are at least a few other people left in the mall. And maybe, just maybe, they will know what the heck is going on!" Zoe smiled back at Madison's enthusiasm. She knew Madison would make a good match, and Emily, at least, wouldn't be a nuisance.

The four girls walked over to where Micah was assigning groups to different areas on the plastic mall map. Grabbing those dry erase markers had been a great idea of Pierce's. As they got in line to receive their orders, Zoe looked carefully at Micah's neat handwriting. He had divided the mall into six equal parts. Three groups would search upstairs and three groups would search downstairs. He was writing the names of each group clearly into the area he wanted them to search. She duly noted that Brittany was in fact searching that area of the mall that had the most fashionable clothing stores. How Brittany could think about clothes at a time like this drove Zoe crazy!

Speaking of clothes, Zoe glanced back to where she saw Malachi talking with Nolan and Ethan. When she saw him return from Macy's she knew Malachi looked different, and now she knew exactly why. Malachi was wearing brand new clothes. Instead of his usual scrubby torn jeans and favorite t-shirt, Malachi was now wearing brand name jeans, new shoes, and a leather jacket. She would have to admit he looked pretty cool. There was no more time to think as Micah turned to Zoe's group and gave them their assignment.

"O.K. why don't you guys search the northern half of the first floor." Micah suggested as he started to pen their names into the section. "Check every single store and bathroom you can find. Also check the employee-only areas behind every store if possible."

Micah finished writing their names and then went on, "When you guys are finished searching your section, radio back to Victoria what you have found. After that, go ahead and make your way to the Sears bedding area that we have designated as our home base. Any questions?"

The four girls were peering closely at the map. Zoe made mental note of the boundaries surrounding section they were assigned to search. Their assigned area was furthest from the food court, so they would want to memorize their duties before heading out.

"Nope, no questions," Madison replied for them all.

Micah dismissed them with a nod before turning to the last group. Several search parties had already headed out on their assignments.

Victoria surprised them by coming up from behind. "Here is your Walkie Talkie and two flashlights. Didn't you already have a flashlight Madison?" Victoria asked.

"Yup" replied Madison.

"Perfect, then your group will have three flashlights. We almost have enough for one per person but not quite. Be sure not to let anyone wander off alone. Use channel number three on the Walkie Talkies. Have any of you used Walkie Talkies before?" Victoria asked and glanced around.

Miel subconsciously raised her hand like they were back in class and Zoe nodded affirmatively. In fact, Zoe was a Walkie Talkie expert. Her family played Walkie Talkie tag every summer at the lake.

"I think you are all set to go. Don't forget to call me when you are finished or if you have found anything important. Good luck!" Victoria mimicked Micah's nod as she turned to equip the last group of kids.

Victoria had given Zoe the Walkie Talkie, so she found a way to hook it to her jeans as they walked across the food court. Some of the food was starting to smell bad and Zoe wondered what it was going to smell like in the morning.

Their group started out at a brisk pace but as soon as they turned the corner of the hall and out of the eyesight of other people, they all automatically slowed down. Suddenly Zoe felt a little nervous about being separated from the group.

"Shall we go down these stairs to the first floor?" Madison suggested and asked at the same time.

"Sure" said Emily. Zoe was surprised that Emily even participated in the conversation. She was curious to learn more about the girl.

"Hey, let's grab some dessert," Miel suggested, then ran over to the Sweet Factory before anyone could argue with her. The store was filled with every type of candy a kid could ever want. The sweets were lined up in large plastic bins covering the store walls. The store reminded Zoe of Charlie and the Chocolate Factory.

Miel had already grabbed some rock candy, a million dollar chocolate bar and a handful of Swedish fish by the time Zoe reached her. Miel was fast.

"Just grab something quick Zoe. Do you guys want anything?" Miel hollered back to Madison and Emily.

"Nah," replied Madison, while Emily only starred at the floor.

"Hurry up Zoe." Miel ordered.

Exasperated with Miel's orders, Zoe grabbed the nearest sucker and some candy necklaces to share in case Madison and Emily changed their minds. She wondered what else she might grab if they returned to this store. She and Miel quickly caught up with Madison and they headed toward the stairs.

Zoe unwrapped her sucker and threw the wrapper in the nearest garbage. Licking on the lollipop gave her pause for reflection. Even if they were only stuck here for a day or two there was every good reason that they should help themselves to the food they need to survive. No one could fault them that. Especially food that was bound to spoil quickly like the warm food they had feasted on tonight.

However, if someone were to just go into the nearest jewelry shop and grab a pair of diamond ear rings? That would be clearly wrong. And what if they were not rescued for a week? Would it be ok for everyone follow Malachi's lead and grab some fresh clothes to wear? Would they be compelled to pick the cheapest possible clothes or to wear anything they liked? These were all interesting questions that Zoe pondered as she sucked on her stolen treat. She followed the girls down the stairs as they headed to the north end of the mall.

"Where do we start searching again?" Miel asked. She had obviously not been paying as much attention as Zoe and Madison. Emily was staring at a store mannequin.

"Abercrombie and Victoria's Secret" Zoe said.

"Victoria's Secret and Abercrombie" Madison said in unison with Zoe. All four of them looked at one another.

"Jinx, you owe me a coke!" Zoe was quickest to interject.

"No problem, I will buy you one when we walk back through the food court!" Madison replied with a wink. Madison could "buy" her a thousand cokes tonight if she wanted to.

They were standing directly between the two stores that marked their starting point. Victoria's Secret was on the left and Abercrombie on the right.

"We should split up into groups of two and search each side of the mall. To be safe, we can meet in the middle after each store to check-in and keep tabs on each other. It is kind of spooky here. I want to shout out 'Hello? Is there anybody out there?' but I am just too creeped out to do it!" Madison was doing all the talking as Miel and Emily seemed to be mute at the moment, if for differing reasons.

Agreeing to the split, Zoe and Miel walked over to Victoria's Secret to start their search. The store was split into two mini-stores connected in the middle by a large arch. They walked in the side that sold perfumes and lotions. It was easy to see that no one was there. A quick look over the sales counter and they had confirmed that there were no people, dead or alive, lurking in the store.

"We need to check the employee area in the back too." Zoe reminded Miel as she started to wander over into the lingerie section.

"Oh yeah," Miel said, and changed her direction to meet up with Zoe. They walked together to the back of the store passing different perfumed lotions. First a cherry blossom scented lotion, then vanilla, then eucalyptus. At the back of the store they walked through a door labeled 'Employees Only.' Zoe always wondered what the employee only section was like and now she would find out.

There was a short hallway, with three open doors. One door led to a small break room with a table, chairs, and microwave. Pamphlets informing workers of their rights were tacked onto the bulletin board, and a sign displaying the current minimum wage hung above the table.

After poking their heads into that room, they walked to the second open door. This room was filled to the brim with tall shelves and overstocked merchandise. Boxes of open and unopened products filled every corner. The room was so crowded it only took a quick glance for them to realize there were no people hiding behind boxes.

They turned around and went down the hall which lead to the employee area behind the lingerie section of the store. Here, they found an even larger room for overstock and a door leading out of

Victoria's Secret to a hallway that connected all the mall stores. Zoe peered into the sparsely lit hallway. She could see several doors, each had the name of the store in black letters stenciled on the back. She shivered, it was even cooler back here compared to the rest of the main mall. Zoe could tell that Miel was peering over her shoulder. She tipped her head to look Miel in the eye.

"Spooky," Miel whispered in her ear. They gave each other a knowing look and shut the door. No people so far.

Heading back into the main store they walked into the lingerie section. This part of the store was larger and crowded with more merchandise than the lotion section; it was going to take a little longer to search. After looking down the spooky back corridor, they decided to stick close together.

"Hey, should we check the dressing rooms as well?" Miel asked as they approached a hallway lined with changing stalls.

Zoe thought for a moment, "Yeah, if we don't do a thorough job we'll worry about it in the morning. We could just call out and see if someone answers, but I would rather check just in case someone is sleeping you know." Or dead, she thought. She could tell Miel was thinking the same thing, but she was unwilling to say it out loud, which is why Zoe said 'sleep' instead of 'dead.'

They walked down the dressing room hall but the first few stalls were locked. They couldn't see under each stall so they couldn't check to see if they were occupied "Do you think we need to find a key and search inside?" Zoe asked.

"Only if we find a key right away, it won't be an efficient use of time if it takes forever to find a key. Let's check the open stalls and look in the cashier area for a key later."

Several rooms were filled with stacks of bras and panties. Zoe laughed out loud and picked up a pink bra with lots of lace and held it out for Miel to see, laughing as she did so.

"Can you imagine if the guys had to search this place!" said Zoe "They would have been so embarrassed, I bet they would not have had the guts to search the dressing rooms!"

Miel laughed with her and held up another funny ensemble from the next dressing room. "We are embarrassed enough as it is, especially for the person that picked out this outfit."

"Well, let's finish up searching the main store and get back outside. I bet Madison and Emily are waiting for us. Let's make sure to check for a key to unlock the remaining dressing rooms." Zoe requested.

The cashier area was easy to search, but they did not find any keys. They quickly looked through the rest of the store, checking behind each rack of clothing and display. Zoe had never shopped at Victoria's Secret before and she was wide eyed.

Sure enough, Emily and Madison were waiting in the mall walkway outside.

"We figured you guys would take twice as long to search Victoria's so we also checked two stores. Did you guys find anything?" Madison asked.

"Nope," Miel spoke up "Although several of the dressing rooms were locked so we can't be 100% sure. But I doubt anyone would be holed up in a locked dressing room."

"Well, let's get going. If each store is going to take this long to search it's going to take all night." Zoe said. She was already getting tired, and it was only a little after eight o'clock.

Checking the next few stores went more quickly as both pairs of girls refined their search techniques. The spookiness of their task also began to wear off as they combed through each store for signs of life. So far, nothing. The dressing rooms in each clothing store were littered with garments, but that was normal at any time of day. There were no indications that people had evacuated the mall in a rush, much less even been there today.

After searching a little over half of their assigned areas, Miel and Zoe were waiting outside of a particularly big store waiting for Madison and Emily to emerge. Miel was sitting on a bench while Zoe paced up and down nearby. Even though she was exhausted, Zoe couldn't settle down, her nerves were wracked. She had hoped they would have found someone, or some clue, as to what happened to all the people.

All of a sudden Zoe heard a sharp sound, followed by several other sharp but faint sounds.

"Miel! I hear something!"

"What?" Miel asked, looking up to see what Zoe was talking about. But Zoe had decided to run down the hall at breakneck speed. She could not believe what she was hearing, it sounded like…like…

Zoe ran as fast as her feet could carry her and the sounds steadily increased in volume. She had to confirm what she was hearing before she would stop. If Zoe was right, she only had a few more stores to go. She knew she was disappearing from Miel's sight as she turned into a shop, but she didn't care. She would explain herself soon enough.

It took her a minute to find out where the noises were coming from, but by the time she had identified the boxes in the corner she could hear Miel's feet pounding behind her.

"Why did you run away?" Miel asked, without even looking at the name of the store Zoe had ran into.

Meanwhile, Zoe had reached down into the box in front of her and pulled up a small bundle that was the source of the sound.

"Look, we're not alone!" Zoe paused to give Miel a closer look at what she was holding. "Puppies!"

CHAPTER 10
DRIFTING

Hope was glad she was in a group with Grace, Victoria and Micah. First, she was happy that all the groups would be checking in with Victoria on her Walkie Talkie. As soon as they found more survivors her group would be the first to know. Second, Micah had made their search area slightly smaller so that they could finish early and be waiting at Sears for everyone else. Their group would start at the movie theater and move east toward Sears. With students like David and Micah taking charge, Hope felt a little less hopeless herself.

A stomachache had been plaguing her since just after the search started. She didn't know if it was her nerves kicking in or the stale chicken nuggets and beef n' bean burrito she ate for dinner. Maybe eating all that fast food hadn't been a good idea after all.

So far, their group hadn't found a single sign of life. They were only ten more stores to explore before they would return to Sears to set up camp. The group approached the Apple store's big clear glass windows, one of the last they needed to check, where Tyler's group was also looking for a landline.

They walked into the bright whiteness of the Apple store to see Malachi and Nolan's fingers flying across iPad screens on opposite sides of the room. Hope could hear Ethan and Tyler talking from behind the genius bar counter.

"Hey guys," Victoria called out gently so as not to startle Malachi and Nolan. "Any luck?"

Tyler popped up from behind the genius bar, responding before Malachi or Nolan could get a word in edgewise. "Nothing! We can't tell if the display products are connected wirelessly or through a landline, so Malachi and Nolan are testing each one for internet access just in case. Either way, the connections must be originating in the back room and distributed via Wi-Fi somewhere in the store. The problem is - we don't have the password to an employee iPhone, so we can't even open these drawers." Tyler dropped behind the counter and out of sight before anyone could respond. Hope smiled, Tyler was indeed a strange character.

Hope saw Ethan slowly stand up and tentatively poke his head out from behind the counter. It was obvious he was not having fun working with Tyler. He looked from Micah to Victoria and then suggested, "I was thinking that we should check the pay phones near the restrooms and the phones at the information desk. Perhaps we can call 911."

Hope heard Tyler grunt from behind the counter as if he thought this was the stupidest idea in the world. She thought it was one of the smartest ideas, and one idea they had all overlooked. Hope decided to speak up. "That's a great idea Ethan. I know this mall pretty well and both of the phones you mentioned are close by. We could go check them out really fast and be back in two minutes flat."

Hope looked at Micah who nodded his approval. Micah would never turn down a good solid logical idea where others (aka Tyler) might object for no reason at all.

"Victoria, Grace and I will finish searching our assigned stores and meet Hope and Ethan back at Sears. Tyler, can you guys handle everything if Ethan goes with Grace to check the phones?" Malachi asked, although his tone did not seek approval.

Tyler gave another grunt from behind the counter but did not show his face. Ethan hurried over to Hope, clearly thankful to leave Tyler's company.

It only took a minute to locate the first payphone next to the restrooms. Hope picked up the phone but there wasn't any dial tone. Even so, she had once heard that 911 worked even when the regular lines were out of service so she gave it a try, but no luck.

"Do you think it would work if we had quarters?" She asked Ethan.

"Um, I don't know," he responded while searching his pockets, "but I don't have any quarters."

"Neither do I," Hope said without having to check her pockets. "Do you think we could break into one of the cash registers and borrow a few?"

"It's worth a try," agreed Ethan.

They ran over to the Sbarro's where they ate dinner earlier that evening and jumped over the counter. Hope tried as she might to open the cash register, but it wouldn't budge. Ethan gently pushed her out of the way, lifted the heavy machine, and stuck his arm underneath.

"If it's an old model, then there might be a switch under here that will open the machine." Ethan continued to feel around the bottom when all of a sudden the cash drawer suddenly flew out, hitting him in the chest.

"Sweet!" he cried. The cash register was stuffed with piles of cash and plenty of quarters.

"Nice job Ethan, how did you know about the lever under the cash register?" Hope asked, looking closely at his face. Most people overlooked Ethan.

He shrugged nonchalantly. "Summers I help out at my grandparents' country store. It is a tiny store with old cash registers, so I thought they might be similar. It was just luck."

"It was good luck," Hope paused and looked up at Ethan thoughtfully. "Here, we might as well take this unopened roll of quarters. It will be easy to carry, and they might come in handy later, especially when we need a gumball from that machine down the hall," Hope suggested as she grabbed the roll of quarters.

They ran back to the pay phone and tried to make a call with the quarters, but it didn't make any difference. The phone was still as silent as the mall. Next, they ran downstairs and tried the payphone on the first floor but no luck. Hope was once again beginning to feel hopeless. People often made fun of her name, but she took it in stride and even made jokes about herself.

"Well, we have one other place we could try. The information desk is right over there. I think they usually have a mall phone both for public and employee use," suggested Hope.

Sure enough, there were two phones at the information desk, one phone on top of the counter for public use and one behind the counter for employee use. Hope let herself into the kiosk while Ethan tried the public phone on the counter. The employee phone was much more sophisticated with lots of automatic dial buttons and fancy features. There was a blinking red light so she knew it must be working. Picking up the receiver she listened for a dial tone. She and Ethan looked up questioningly at each other but both shook their heads in disappointment. Nothing, no dial tone, no outside access – they were utterly and completely cut off from the outside world.

Hope looked more closely at the blinking red light. It was coming from a button marked with an envelope and must be a saved "message." She picked up the receiver once again and pushed the blinking red envelope.

"You have 1 new message" the machine voice greeted her, "press 1 to listen to new messages, press 2 to listen to…"

Hope pressed 1 while simultaneously pressing down the speaker button so Ethan could hear as well.

"New message received at 4:08 p.m," echoed the recording throughout the mall walkway. Then they heard the gruff voice of a man. "Carter? This is Matt from down in receivables. We are having some problems on the loading dock with all this snow. Some of the smaller trucks are getting stuck and we may need a tow. Will you get me the number of the Devithan Trading company so I can call and see what they want me to do about the trucks? They may be able to bring in the merchandise by foot. It would be messy and take awhile, but I don't think I can allow them to bring the truck up to the loading dock without better snow tires. Thanks." The call ended abruptly.

"Well, now we know the mall was having trouble with the snow, but it doesn't really let us know why everyone disappeared or why there is thirty feet of snow outside. It also doesn't sound like there was much snow outside at 4:08. Does that mean that thirty feet fell in one hour? Impossible! We were out of the movie by 5:15 at the latest!" Hope surmised. She set down the receiver and the light turned off. No new messages.

"Let's head to Sears to meet the others, they'll probably be done searching soon." Ethan suggested. Hope left the information kiosk and followed him down the hall to Sears. Female voices filtered out of the Guess shop as they passed by.

"Hey, I think that's Brittany and her group." Hope told Ethan. She grabbed his arm and pulled him inside the store before he could object. It was easy to locate Brittany, Lindsey, Molly and Alliyah in the back corner.

The Guess store had white mannequins, bright lights, and wide aisles. The shoes were displayed stylishly in the corner. A few streamlined black shelves laid on a white background held up the most gorgeous shoes.

Brittany was modeling a single red stiletto in the mirror while Molly was trying to force her large foot into a dark leather shoe. It was obvious the girls were not "searching" for missing people. Hope decided to ignore this fact and be nice to them anyway.

"Hey there," Hope greeted them casually to get their attention. "Did you guys find anything yet?" she asked, even though she knew the answer already. No one would be trying on shoes if they had actually found another person stuck in the mall.

Brittany and Molly jumped at the sound of her voice while

Lindsey didn't even hear her. Molly hesitated, froze in the act of trying on shoes, and looked to Brittany for guidance.

Brittany didn't hesitate at all. "Nope, we haven't found a single thing and we have searched every store from Barnes and Noble to here. I don't think there is anyone else in this forsaken place." She paused and gave her foot another look in the mirror. "What do you think guys? Is red my color?" she asked mockingly.

Ethan's jaw dropped at Brittany's comment. Even though Hope didn't consider Brittany to be very beautiful, guys seemed attracted to her bossiness. Or maybe they were just scared of her. Hope didn't understand how boys worked or why they acted like they did. It seemed Ethan was no exception.

"Yeah, Brittany, they look good on yo-you," Ethan stuttered on the last word. Hope gave him a scathing look in her head while keeping her face impassive. Didn't he know Brittany was being completely facetious?

Hope decided to ignore Brittany's rude manner and not respond to her comment directly. "I agree, I don't think anyone else was left behind. Like David said, I expect this is a dream and we haven't woken up yet. Besides," Hope added with a smile, "Isn't it every kid's dream to have a whole mall entirely to themselves? Just think, if this is only a dream we can do whatever we want in this mall. Eat all the food we want, wear any clothes we want, and have hundreds of pairs of shoes with no consequences whatsoever."

Brittany smiled back at this comment. Good, thought Hope. She managed to strike a chord with the girl. She may not really like Brittany, but she could be as intimidated as the rest of the kids. Hope preferred to be on Brittany's good side.

"Even if it isn't a dream we can do as we please! There are thirty feet of snow outside." Brittany retorted with distain.

Hope sighed inwardly, Brittany was in one of her moods, so there was no reason to stick around and chat. "Well girls, Ethan and I are supposed to be meeting Micah, Victoria, and Grace at Sears. We'll see you guys when you're finished searching your section." Hope grabbed Ethan's arm and dragged him with her, otherwise he would have stood staring at the girls forever. He seemed to be in a daze as they marched out of the Guess store toward Sears.

"You ok?" Hope asked Ethan to elicit a response.

"Uh, yeah," was all he could reply. He shook his head back and forth as if in a fog. Why didn't guys ever do that when they talked to her? It was like she didn't exist. In that way, she and Ethan were very similar - they were always ignored by everyone.

She counted the storefronts as they made their way to Sears. 1,2,3,4,5, 6,7,8,9,10,11 and home. They walked side-by-side into the big box store. As they entered the store she noted that the bath section was to their left, the bedding to their right, and house wares straight ahead. Stopping as soon as they hit the intersection she peered closely down the walkways. Far to the right she could see a corner of the store where they kept the model beds.

"We didn't make plans with Victoria and we don't have a Walkie-talkie but I think we should wait in the bed area. Isn't that why we choose Sears in the first place? Because it would have a place for us to crash if we stay here all night?" She looked to Ethan, waiting expectantly for an answer.

Like a person who isn't used to having people ask for his opinion, Ethan didn't seem to be listening closely to her. Makes sense. If people don't listen to you, you tend not to listen to people. Rubbing her hands together for warmth, Hope put her hot palm on Ethan's shoulder and repeated her question. Promising herself that she would listen carefully to his answer.

After getting his attention, Ethan did listen attentively to her. He agreed that it was a good plan and so they walked together in silence to the model beds. Zoe had been right, Sears had lots of beds with more than enough room to sleep the entire class. Some people would have to share the larger beds, but she doubted everyone would sleep at the same time.

Hope and Ethan stood there for awhile just looking around the quiet store. The television section was south of where they were standing and they could hear several different movies playing. It was eerie. She decided to wait for Ethan to make the first comment.

"Well, we might be here for awhile. What do you say we walk over to the electronics section and watch a movie while we wait?" Ethan suggested.

Hope thought for a minute before making her reply, "Great idea. Let me leave a quick note letting Micah know we are here in case they can't see us from this angle. I wouldn't want them to worry." Hope ran over to the nearest cashier and looked for some paper and a marker. Finding both easily, she scribbled a note in large black letters and left in on the first bed.

When they arrived in the electronics section they discovered that about half of the screens were playing movies and the other half were just static. "I wonder why half of these are static?" Hope thought out loud.

"I think it is because they may have been tuned to a local television station and the rest were playing DVD's. I mean, if cell phone service and phone land lines are down then it makes sense that local television would also be down." Ethan replied. "But wait, local television!" He seemed to be rethinking his comment about local T.V. Ethan paused and ran over to the nearest television. He fiddled with the buttons and looked around until he found the remote control. He then tried to go through several channels before giving up.

"I was hoping that maybe local television channels were making it through. Then we could look up the news and see what is going on in the outside world, but I think I was right about it being cut off just like the Wi-Fi." Ethan looked dejected. Every possibility of escape seemed to be a dead end.

"Well, I guess all we can do is wait." Hope gave him a weak smile as she sat down on a large leather sofa facing the televisions. She realized that before they could watch a movie they would have to turn off all the others. "What kind of movie would you like to watch Ethan?" There were three movies on at the moment, one was a cartoon, one a horror film, and the third a romantic comedy. None of them appealed to Hope.

"The cartoon," Ethan replied with a rueful smile. They started turning off the television sets one by one, leaving the cartoon on the largest screen closest to the leather couch. Finished, they both sat down and Hope let out a big yawn.

"Well perhaps I am a little tired." Hope said.

They had only watched for a few minutes before they heard soft footsteps behind them. Even though she was not startled to hear someone approaching, it did make her jump involuntarily. Hope turned around to see Grace looking at all the empty televisions.

"Thanks for leaving that note," Grace began leaning over the back of the couch, "we're gathering near the beds. Micah is wondering if you would come back and meet with him, he wants to hear your report," said Grace.

Standing up with another stretch and a great big yawn, Hope pulled herself up off the couch. Ethan was a little slower to get up as well. He must have been as tired as she.

"Thanks for coming to get us Grace, we were not sure how long it would take you guys to get back," then Hope continued, "We didn't have any luck. None of the phones were working."

Grace nodded. "I didn't expect them to be working. And if they were, I would have thought you guys would be running to tell us the news. We didn't have any luck on our end either."

Hope and Grace started walking back to the bed section while Ethan watched a few last scenes of the animated film before turning to follow them. They could see Micah and Victoria sitting on the edge of a bed talking loudly into the Walkie-talkie. As soon as Hope noticed their excitement, she quickened her pace so she could get closer and hear what they were saying.

"Repeat, what did you find?" Victoria asked again in a loud voice, obviously struggling with the Walkie-talkie buttons.

"We're not alone!" the static accompanying Zoe's voice was hampering the signal. "We were searching the northeast corner and we found puppies!"

"Repeat, you found some puppies?" Victoria furrowed her brows at Micah. "puppies" she mouthed.

"Yeah, puppies at that store that sells all things dog. They are sooo cute!" Zoe continued to talk but Victoria interrupted her.

"You mean there are five dogs left in the mall?" she asked redundantly. It was obvious there were five canines in the mall. It was just taking a minute to sink in. There may not be any people left in the mall, but there were animals.

"Yes! We still have a bunch of stores to finish searching, but we will radio again when we start heading back. Maybe we will bring the puppies with us." Zoe radioed back.

Victoria shrugged her shoulders and responded, "Sounds good. Talk to you soon."

"Well, now that I think of it, there is also a reptile shop on the second floor. We may not only have puppies but turtles, lizards, and snakes too." Micah added logically.

Hope shivered at the thought. She remembered the reptile store and there were more than just snakes. She remembered seeing several types of tarantulas when she visited that store with her brother. Hope imagined a mall full of hungry reptiles roaming the halls. Yikes!

"Victoria! Micah! Are you there?" Everyone surrounded Victoria and her Walkie Talkie. The voice on the other end of the radio was breathless and excited. Hope had not been expecting another communication so soon after Zoe's call.

"Yeah, this is Victoria and Micah. What do you have to report?" Victoria asked in a clear voice. She was finally getting a hang of the Walkie Talkies.

"We just found someone! Cody was walking along the upper level next to Zumiez and he saw someone down the hall. Cody and Luke went to check it out. Tanner and I are catching up with them right now." David's voice was accompanied with huffs, puffs, and the pounding of feet. He and Tanner must be running very quickly.

"Stay on the Walkie Talkie until you contact them David,"

Micah ordered, his face lit up. Micah had been sure they were not alone in the mall and now there would be proof.

"Sounds good," David replied, still huffing and puffing.

Hope sat down on the bed next to Victoria to hear what happened next. Grace and Ethan were standing next to Micah looking at the Walkie Talkie as though they could see a visual of the situation. They all sat poised, listening to the intermittent sound of footsteps.

Everyone held their breath as a few tense minutes passed. David hadn't taken his hand off the Walkie Talkie talk button so Victoria wasn't able to ask him any questions. Finally, they heard voices. David was asking Cody what had happened. Cody was talking too quickly, his voice breaking up every few words. From what they could pick up, Cody had not been able to contact the person. Or maybe there hadn't been a person in the first place. Hope could hear Cody and David arguing but she couldn't make out what they were saying. Finally, David's voice addressed the Walkie-Talkie.

"False alarm. Cody thought he saw someone but it must have been a mannequin."

"I did too…" Cody's voice was cut off before he could finish interrupting David's report.

Victoria waited a second to see if they were finished talking. The Walkie-Talkie remained silent. Micah held his hand out, beckoning Victoria to hand him the Walkie-Talkie.

"David, can you hear me? It's Micah," he spoke into the small black box.

Micah took his hand off the talk button and waited patiently.

"Yeah Micah, this is David. Cody thought he saw a person, but when he and Luke ran down to make contact they couldn't find anyone. Either Cody was seeing things…" here David paused suspiciously, "…or the person ran away. I don't know why anyone would want to run away? No one else saw anything. I think Cody is just acting crazy." David finished.

Hope could still hear Cody arguing in the background. This was strange. Cody and David were good friends. And although they would argue in jest she had never heard them argue with such vehemence. She wondered if the Walkie Talkies made their voices sound that way.

"No problem. Just finish searching and walk down to Sears when you are done. Keep your eyes peeled in case Cody really did see someone," Micah replied. Hope could tell he was disappointed.

"Over and out," David responded.

It was eerily quiet after that. The entire night Hope had been vacillating between a weird sort of calm and a totally freaked out disposition. The empty store was more then she could stand. Looking around she counted the model beds on display. There were twenty-six models that were full size, and two twins beds. How strange, there were exactly enough beds for each student to have their own bed.

Despite her nervousness she could tell the long day had taken its toll. Victoria and Micah were busy reviewing the search parties and the map they had copied down, so Hope decided to take a closer look around the bedding area. She was almost ready to make herself comfortable and take a nap. Besides, Victoria and Micah appeared to have everything under control and there didn't appear to be anything she could do to help them at this time.

The display beds were arranged in a large square with a row of beds running down the middle. There were three walls surrounding the beds which made it feel private compared to the large open feeling in the rest of the store. She looked at the sign listing the prices for the different sizes of bed. King, queen, full, and twin. Hope looked up at the beds again. They were all the same size but she couldn't tell if they were full beds or queens. The beds were certainly not king size, they must make the sample beds small on purpose so the store could stock a greater variety.

She sat on the first bed and tested it for comfort. Each display bed had a body pillow covered in a satin like material at the top of the bed, and a long strip of matching material at the foot of the bed.

As she lay down to test the bed she realized the strip at the bottom protected the bed from dirty feet. Hope checked her shoes out of habit, but they were perfectly clean.

The bed was really comfortable, much nicer than her bed back home. But then, they must keep only the best for display purposes, and her bed at home was ten years old, a hand me down from her older sister.

Hope tried a few more beds. They were all pretty much the same except for those that had a thick layer of pillow top as those were the comfiest. She was now on the opposite side of the room from her friends, looking back over her shoulder she could see Ethan and Grace actively engaged with Micah. She wondered what they were talking about and wondered if she should get back, but was too tired to worry about it.

Hope rolled over on her side and closed her eyes for a minute to let the events of the day melt away. It had started out pretty normal. She awoke on her old lumpy bed to an early but familiar alarm. Then stretched, dressed, grabbed her backpack, and headed to school to meet up with the field trip bus. In fact, other than it being a field trip day, everything had been extremely normal until the end of the movie. Hope remembered that as the credits were rolling she had begun to get a queasy stomachache. While at first she attributed it to soda and candy, now she wondered if it was just a precursor of the events to come.

Hope wrinkled her nose. The bed she was lying on smelled funny, not bad necessarily, but an unfamiliar new bed smell. Opening her eyes she yawned and stretched just like she had earlier this morning. She was tired of worrying about the predicament they were in, and she just wanted to fall asleep and forget everything. Maybe if she fell asleep she would wake up in her own bed back home in good old Canada.

Hope looked back again at her friends. They were still talking excitedly about something or another, they were far enough away she couldn't make out what they were saying. Deciding that they would not miss her, Hope got up and quietly started walking down the aisle of beds toward the bedding section. She wouldn't go far, but she wanted to pick out a pillow and comforter to make the bed a little more homey. Then, if no one else minded, she would take a nap while they waited for the other search parties to return.

Not wanting to go far, Hope went down the first aisle that displayed comforters. She passed by several down and down alternative comforters. They ranged in price from thirty to two hundred dollars. A little allergic to goose down, Hope decided to skip those for now and see what else Sears had to offer.

Next came the bedding sets, complete with comforters, pillowcases, and bed shams. Of course, she didn't need anything so fancy, but a lilac colored set caught her eye. It was exactly the kind of bed cover she would choose if she could create her dream bedroom.

She unzipped a corner of the plastic case and fingered the soft colored material. It was sleek feeling, with gorgeous embroidered flowers lining the edges in black thread. Ah, well. She was pretty sure she would be ridiculed if she opened up an expensive set of bedding, better settle for something less extravagant. Yet, as Hope turned away, she promised herself she would someday return and buy the most lavish bedroom set available.

Pillow tops and mattress covers filled the next two aisles, and then finally she found the cheap blankets and comforters. Running her hand along the different fabrics she choose a dark blue micro plush blanket. It was thick and felt warm against her skin. Picking it up by the ribbon wrapped around it, she swung it back and forth as she continued to search. In addition to the blanket she wanted to get a pillow, and possibly some sheets. Either she would need to wrap herself in the blanket like a hot dog or get some sheets and make a proper bed.

The pillows and sheets were located on the other side of the main entrance to Sears. Hope slowed down and peeked her head around the corner looking out into the main mall. She was peering out from behind one of those fake half beds that was used to display bed sets. For a second she was distracted by the beautiful bed set, but then her eyes were drawn back to the lonely quiet mall. It looked scary out there. Even though all the lights were still on, she could see the black skylight stretching forever into the darkness.

It took courage for her to take the first step across the walkway, as soon as her foot crossed the imaginary line that separated the shopping area from the walkway, Hope bolted across as fast as she could and plunged into the relative safety of the pillow aisle.

She gulped, and regained her composure. There were lots of pillows to choose from, but she was too tired to comparison shop so she just grabbed one that looked decent. This led her right into the sheet aisle. She might as well get a set of sheets so she could use the pillowcase, and if she decided not to use the sheets on the bed it would be no big deal, she would return the package to the right aisle. After all, she was just borrowing all this stuff right?

Hope didn't know anything about sheets. The sign in front of her said 800 thread count, whatever that was. She looked for a nice dark blue to match her blanket and grabbed a queen size set. If the sheets were too big she could just tuck them in around the edges.

She returned to the display beds the same way she came, speeding across the main entrance, past the comforters, and into the back corner. She glanced back at her friends and made eye contact with Victoria who was talking to Micah. Hope wondered if she had worried Victoria by disappearing like that. She decided to set down her blanket, pillow, and sheets before walking back to her friends.

Victoria was still watching her closely as she approached, but her eyes were smiling.

"Feeling a little tired Hope?" Victoria asked.

"Yeah," Hope responded a little sheepishly at first, but when Victoria continued to smile she didn't feel so bad. "I grabbed a blanket n' stuff so I could lay down for awhile. Do you guys need any help before I take a nap?" Hope still felt bad. What if Victoria felt like a nap? None of them looked surprised to see her return, so they must not have noticed when she left. Hope wondered why they hadn't called out to her, but then she shrugged. What did it matter? She was tired and they were all just sitting there waiting.

"Nah, we are just waiting around for everyone to check-in and return. So far three groups are on their way and should be here any minute. David's groups is taking a little longer and we haven't heard back again from Miel's group. Go ahead and take a nap. We will be sure to wake you up if anything changes," replied Victoria.

"Thanks, but be sure to wake me okay?" Hope responded. Victoria nodded at her reassuringly, so she made her way back to the bed in the corner.

First she opened the plastic bag containing the sheets and pillowcases. Pulling out the new sheets Hope shook them out so they cascaded down, unfolding themselves. A cardboard square that held the center firm fell out onto the ground. The sheets were creased in a neat square pattern that normally would be washed away before use. Hope laughed to herself. Sears must have a million washing machines but none of them were hooked up. Even if she wanted to wash these sheets it would be impossible. Unless she took them down to the creek with a bar of soap…

Hope was starting to hallucinate she must be that tired. Shaking out the sheets she looked around to make a final decision on which bed to claim. She had first pick! The bed in the corner would give her a good view of the entire room, sleeping in that bed would feel a little safer than those right next to the main aisles.

Having made up her mind, Hope whipped the fitted sheet over the bed in one quick motion. Whoa, the queen sized sheet was quite a bit bigger than the bed. They must make display beds much smaller, she thought to herself, just like the half-beds that were used to display bedding near the main entrance.

Tucking in the sheet made it fit a little more snuggly than her first try. She threw on the top sheet and put the pillowcase on her pillow. Almost time to sleep! The blue blanket did not have a plastic cover, but was instead tied up with a ribbon. Tugging at the knot, Hope untied the ribbon easily and pulled out the blanket which she then spread over the sheets. She took off her jacket and kicked off her shoes before diving into the soft sea of blue.

Even though she had sheets, Hope wanted that tucked in feeling. So she wrapped the sheets and blankets tightly around her body, tucking in the edges. Closing her eyes she listened to the sounds around her. Now that she was still, she could almost make out her friends voices from across the room. Micah was making plans for tomorrow. Sleep did not come to her immediately, but she was so overwhelmed that closing her eyes was a logical choice. At some point she fell into a deep sleep.

Several times throughout the night Hope awoke groggily and peeked through her eyelids. Once, she saw a larger group of students surrounding Micah and Victoria. Another time she saw a variety of colored sleeping bags dotting the beds around her. Good, other people were sleeping too.

Another time she could have sworn she saw a little golden puppy running across a nearby bed. Didn't Zoe find some puppies? Her groggy mind asked, but before she could answer her own question she was asleep again. It was not until several hours later that Hope was able to rouse herself from the deep slumber.

She opened her eyes wide and looked around the room, but kept her body still. She did not feel like getting up, stretching, or letting anyone know she was awake, she just wanted to look around.

Almost everyone had a sleeping bag or blanket like hers spread out on a bed. Sure enough her count was right on. Twenty-eight students and twenty-eight beds. At first glance, everyone appeared to be asleep, so it must be late at night. After a few more minutes of listening her ears picked up some quiet whispering. Not everyone was asleep.

Her eyes adjusting to the bright light, Hope continued to scan the room. It was then that she focused on an image close to her. Miel and Zoe had settled down into separate sleeping bags on the bed next to Hope. Cuddled right in between them, Hope had a clear look at the cutest puppy dog she had ever seen. He or she was laying sprawled between the two girls, front paws crossed.

Hope smiled. Her brain had spent the night processing yesterday's strange events. One thing was clear. Today they were stuck in a mall, buried under thirty feet of snow, with the cutest puppy in the world, with the electricity still working. However strange, life could be much worse. And they still had 'Hope' she thought to herself as she drifted off to sleep again.

ABOUT THE AUTHOR

I hate shopping. Always have and probably always will. But this story stuck with me since I was very young and I knew there was much more to it that simply fulfilling the universal desire to have everything. Material goods are a gift, a privilege, and an opportunity not much different that the honor of loving our Mother Earth. So I write about the mall but I do so because our spiritual being seems so independent from the physical world around us…and yet…we can make magic with "stuff" just as surely as our imaginations can create new realities.

The moral of the story is Dream. Dream with your heart. Dream with your head. Dream with your hands.

Made in the USA
Lexington, KY
06 April 2017